IN THE QUARTER

Robert W. Chambers

1st WORLD
LIBRARY
Literary Society

In the Quarter

Robert W. Chambers

© 1st World Library – Literary Society, 2004
PO Box 2211
Fairfield, IA 52556
www.1stworldlibrary.org
First Edition

LCCN: 2004195351

Softcover ISBN: 1-4218-0185-X
Hardcover ISBN: 1-4218-0085-3
eBook ISBN: 1-4218-0285-6

Purchase *"In the Quarter"*
as a traditional bound book at:
www.1stWorldLibrary.org/purchase.asp?ISBN=1-4218-0185-X

1st World Library Literary Society is a nonprofit
organization dedicated to promoting literacy by:

- Creating a free internet library accessible from any
  computer worldwide.
- Hosting writing competitions and offering book
  publishing scholarships.

Readers interested in supporting literacy
through sponsorship, donations or
membership please contact:
literacy@1stworldlibrary.org
Check us out at: www.1stworldlibrary.ORG
and start downloading free ebooks today.

In the Quarter
contributed by Tim, Ed & Rodney
in support of
1st World Library Literary Society

One

One evening in May, 1888, the Café des Écoles was even more crowded and more noisy than usual. The marble-topped tables were wet with beer and the din was appalling. Someone shouted to make himself heard.

"Any more news from the Salon?"

"Yes," said Elliott, "Thaxton's in with a number three. Rhodes is out and takes it hard. Clifford's out too, and takes it - "

A voice began to chant:

> Je n'sais comment faire,
>   Comment concillier
> Ma maitresse et mon père,
>   Le Code et Bullier.

"Drop it! Oh, drop it!" growled Rhodes, and sent a handful of billiard chalk at the singer.

Mr Clifford returned a volley of the Café spoons, and continued:

> Mais c'que je trouve de plus bête,
>   C'est qu' i' faut financer
> Avec ma belle galette,
>   J'aimerai mieux m'amuser.

Several other voices took up the refrain, lamenting the difficulty of reconciling their filial duties with balls at Bullier's, and protesting that they would rather amuse themselves than consider financial questions. Rhodes sipped his curaçoa sulkily.

"The longer I live in the Latin Quarter," he said to his neighbor, "the less certain I feel about a place of future punishment. It would be so tame after this." Then, reverting to his grievance, he added, "The slaughter this year at the Salon is awful."

Reginald Gethryn stirred nervously but did not speak.

"Have a game, Rex?" called Clifford, waving a cue.

Gethryn shook his head, and reaching for a soiled copy of the Figaro, glanced listlessly over its contents. He sighed and turned his paper impatiently. Rhodes echoed the sigh.

"What's at the theaters?"

"Same as last week, excepting at the Gaieté. They've put on `La Belle Hélène' there."

"Oh! Belle Hélène!" cried Clifford.

> Tzing! la! la! Tzing! la! la!
>   C'est avec ces dames qu' Oreste
> Fait danser l'argent de Papa!

Robert W. Chambers

Rhodes began to growl again.

"I shouldn't think you'd feel like gibbering that rot tonight."

Clifford smiled sweetly and patted him on the head. "Tzing! la! la! My shot, Elliott?"

"Tzing! la! la!" laughed Thaxton, "That's Clifford's biography in three words."

Clifford repeated the refrain and winked impudently at the pretty bookkeeper behind her railing. She, alas! returned it with a blush.

Gethryn rose restlessly and went over to another table where a man, young, but older than himself, sat, looking comfortable.

"Braith," he began, trying to speak indifferently, "any news of my fate?"

The other man finished his beer and then answered carelessly, "No." But catching sight of Gethryn's face he added, with a laugh:

"Look here, Rex, you've got to stop this moping."

"I'm not moping," said Rex, coloring up.

"What do you call it, then?" Braith spoke with some sharpness, but continued kindly, "You know I've been through it all. Ten years ago, when I sent in my first picture, I confess to you I suffered the torments of the damned until - "

"Until?"

"Until they sent me my card. The color was green."

"But I thought a green card meant `not admitted.'"

"It does. I received three in three years."

"Do you mean you were thrown out three years in succession?"

Braith knocked the ashes out of his pipe. "I gave up smoking for those three years."

"You?"

Braith filled his pipe tenderly. "I was very poor," he said.

"If I had half your sand!" sighed Rex.

"You have, and something more that the rest of us have not. But you are very young yet."

This time Gethryn colored with surprise and pleasure. In all their long and close friendship Braith had never before given him any other encouragement than a cool, "Go ahead!"

He continued: "Your curse thus far has been want of steady application, and moreover you're too easily scared. No matter what happens this time, no knocking under!"

"Oh, I'm not going to knock under. No more is Clifford, it seems," Rex added with a laugh, as Clifford threw down his cue and took a step of the devil's quadrille.

"Oh! Elliott!" he crowed, "what's the matter with you?"

Elliott turned and punched a sleepy waiter in the ribs.

"Emile - two bocks!"

The waiter jumped up and rubbed his eyes. "What is it, monsieur?" he snapped.

Elliott repeated the order and they strolled off toward a table. As Clifford came lounging by, Carleton said, "I hear you lead with a number one at the Salon."

"Right, I'm the first to be fired."

"He's calm now," said Elliott, "but you should have seen him yesterday when the green card came."

"Well, yes. I discoursed a little in several languages."

"After he had used up his English profanity, he called the Jury names in French, German and Spanish. The German stuck, but came out at last like a cork out of a bottle - "

"Or a bung out of a barrel."

"These comparisons are as offensive as they are unjust," said Clifford.

"Quite so," said Braith. "Here's the waiter with your beer."

"What number did you get, Braith?" asked Rhodes, who couldn't keep his mind off the subject and made no pretense of trying.

"Three," answered Braith.

There was a howl, and all began to talk at once.

"There's justice for you!" "No justice for Americans!" "Serves us right for our tariff!" "Are Frenchmen going to give us all the advantages of their schools and honors besides while we do all we can to keep their pictures out of our markets?"

"No, we don't, either! Tariff only keeps out the sweepings of the studios - "

"If there were no duty on pictures the States would be flooded with trash."

"Take it off!" cried one.

"Make it higher!" shouted another.

"Idiots!" growled Rhodes. "Let 'em flood the country with bad work as well as good. It will educate the people, and the day will come when all good work will stand an equal chance - be it French or be it American."

"True," said Clifford, "Let's all have a bock. Where's Rex?"

But Gethryn had slipped out in the confusion. Quitting the Café des Écoles, he sauntered across the street, and turning through the Rue de Vaugirard, entered the rue

Monsieur le Prince. He crossed the dim courtyard of his hôtel, and taking a key and a candle from the lodge of the Concierge, started to mount the six flights to his bedroom and studio. He felt irritable and fagged, and it did not make matters better when he found, on reaching his own door, that he had taken the wrong key. Nor did it ease his mind to fling the key over the banisters into the silent stone hallway below. He leaned sulkily over the railing and listened to it ring and clink down into the darkness, and then, with a brief but vigorous word, he turned and forced in his door with a crash. Two bull pups which had flown at him with portentous growls and yelps of menace now gamboled idiotically about him, writhing with antici-pation of caresses, and a gray and scarlet parrot, rudely awakened, launched forth upon a musical effort resembling the song of a rusty cart-wheel.

"Oh, you infernal bird!" murmured the master, lighting his candle with one hand and fondling the pups with the other. "There, there, puppies, run away!" he added, rolling the ecstatic pups into a sort of dog divan, where they curled themselves down at last and subsided with squirms and wriggles, gurgling affection.

Gethryn lighted a lamp and then a cigarette. Then, blowing out the candle, he sat down with a sigh. His eyes fell on the parrot. It annoyed him that the parrot should immediately turn over and look at him upside down. It also annoyed him that "Satan," an evil-looking raven, was evidently preparing to descend from his perch and worry "Mrs Gummidge."

"Mrs Gummidge" was the name Clifford had given to a large sad-eyed white tabby who now lay dozing upon a panther skin.

"Satan!" said Gethryn. The bird checked his sinister preparations and eyed his master. "Don't," said the young man.

Satan weighed his chances and came to the conclusion that he could swoop down, nip Mrs Gummidge, and get back to his bust of Pallas without being caught. He tried it, but his master was too quick for him, and foiled, he lay sullenly in Gethryn's hands, his two long claws projecting helplessly between the brown fists of his master.

"Oh, you fiend!" muttered Rex, taking him toward a wicker basket, which he hated. "Solitary confinement for you, my boy."

"Double, double, toil and trouble," croaked the parrot.

Gethryn started nervously and shut him inside the cage, a regal gilt structure with "Shakespeare" printed over the door. Then, replacing the agitated Gummidge on her panther skin, he sat down once more and lighted another cigarette.

His picture. He could think of nothing else. It was a serious matter with Gethryn. Admitted to the Salon meant three more years' study in Paris. Failure, and back he must go to New York.

The personal income of Reginald Gethryn amounted to the magnificent sum of two hundred and fifty dollars. To this, his aunt, Miss Celestia Gethryn, added nine hundred and fifty dollars more. This gave him a sum of twelve hundred dollars a year to live on and study in Paris. It was not a large sum, but it was princely when compared to the amount on which many a talented fellow subsists, spending his best years in a foul atmosphere of paint and tobacco, ill fed, ill clothed, scarcely warmed at all, often sick in mind and body, attaining his first scant measure of success just as his overtaxed powers give way.

Gethryn's aunt, his only surviving relative, had recently written him one of her ponderous letters. He took it from his pocket and began to read it again, for the fourth time.

> You have now been in Paris three years, and as yet I have seen no results. You should be earning your own living, but instead you are still dependent upon me. You are welcome to all the assistance I can give you, in reason, but I expect that you will have something to show for all the money I expend upon you. Why are you not making a handsome income and a splendid reputation, like Mr Spinder?

The artist named was thirty-five and had been in Paris fifteen years. Gethryn was twenty-two and had been studying three years.

> Why are you not doing beautiful things, like Mr Mousely? I'm told he gets a thousand dollars for a little sketch.

Rex groaned. Mr Mousely could neither draw nor paint, but he made stories of babies' deathbeds on squares of canvas with china angels solidly suspended from the ceiling of the nursery, pointing upward, and he gave them titles out of the hymnbook, which caused them to be bought with eagerness by all the members of the congregation to which his family belonged.

The letter proceeded:

> I am told by many reliable persons that three years abroad is more than enough for a thorough art education. If no results are attained at the end of that time, there is only one of two conclusions to be drawn. Either you have no talent, or you are wasting your time. I shall wait until the next Salon before I come to a decision. If then you have a picture accepted and if it shows no trace of the immorality which is rife in Paris, I will continue your allowance for three years more; this, however, on condition that you have a picture in the Salon each year. If you fail again this year, I shall insist upon your coming home at once.

Why Gethryn should want to read this letter four times, when one perusal of it had been more than enough, no one, least of all himself, could have told. He sat now crushing it in is hand, tasting all the bitterness that is stored up for a sensitive artist tied by fate to an omniscient Philistine who feeds his body with bread and his soul with instruction about art and behavior.

Presently he mastered the black mood which came near being too much for him, his face cleared and he leaned back, quietly smoking. From the rug rose a muffled rumbling where Mrs Gummidge dozed in peace. The clock ticked sharply. A mouse dropped silently from the window curtain and scuttled away unmarked.

The pups lay in a soft heap. The parrot no longer hung head downward, but rested in his cage in a normal position, one eye fixed steadily on Gethryn, the other sheathed in a bluish-white eyelid, every wrinkle of which spoke scorn of men and things.

For some time Gethryn had been half-conscious of a piano sounding on the floor below. It suddenly struck him now that the apartment under his, which had been long vacant, must have found an occupant.

"Idiots!" he grumbled. "Playing at midnight! That will have to stop. Singing too! We'll see about that!"

The singing continued, a girl's voice, only passably trained, but certainly fresh and sweet.

Gethryn began to listen, reluctantly and ungraciously. There was a pause. "Now she's going to stop. It's time," he muttered. But the piano began again - a short prelude which he knew, and the voice was soon in the midst of the Dream Song from "La Belle Hélène."

Gethryn rose and walked to his window, threw it open and leaned out. An April night, soft and delicious. The air was heavy with perfume from the pink and white chestnut blossoms. The roof dripped with moisture. Far down in the dark court the gas-jets flickered and flared. From the distance came the softened rumble of a midnight cab, which, drawing nearer and nearer and passing the hôtel with a rollicking rattle of wheels and laughing voices, died away on the smooth pavement by the Luxembourg Gardens. The voice had stopped capriciously in the middle of the song. Gethryn turned back into the room whistling the air. His eye fell on Satan sitting behind his bars in crumpled malice.

"Poor old chap," laughed the master, "want to come out and hop around a bit? Here, Gummidge, we'll remove temptation out of his way," and he lifted the docile tabby, who increased the timbre of her song to an ecstatic squeal at his touch, and opening his bedroom door, gently deposited her on his softest blankets. He then reinstated the raven on his bust of Pallas, and Satan watched him from thence warily as he fussed about the studio, sorting brushes, scraping a neglected palette, taking down a dressing gown, drawing on a pair of easy slippers, opening his door and depositing his boots outside. When he returned the music had begun again.

"What on earth does she mean by singing at a quarter to one o'clock?" he thought, and went once more to the window. "Why - that is really beautiful."

Oui! c'est un rêve, Oui! c'est un rêve doux d'amour.
  La nuit lui prête son mystère,
Il doit finir - il doit finir avec le jour.

The song of Hélène ceased. Gethryn leaned out and gazed down at the lighted windows under his. Suddenly the light went out. He heard someone open the window, and straining his eyes, could just discern the dim outline of a head and shoulders, unmistakably those of a girl. She had perched herself on the window-sill. Presently she began to hum the air, then to sing it softly. Gethryn waited until the words came again:

Oui, c'est un rêve -

and then struck in with a very sweet baritone:

Oui, c'est un rêve -

She never moved, but her voice swelled out fresh and clear in answer to his, and a really charming duet came to a delightful finish. Then she looked up. Gethryn was reckless now.

"Shall it be, then, only a dream?" he laughed. Was it his fate that made him lean out and whisper, "Is it, then, only a dream, Hélène?"

There was nothing but the rustling of the chestnut branches to answer his folly. Not another sound. He was half inclined to shut his window and go in, well satisfied with the silence and beginning to feel sleepy. All at once from below came a faint laugh, and as he leaned out he caught the words:

"Paris, Hélène bids you good night!"

"Ah, Belle Hélène!" - he began, but was cut short by the violent opening of a window opposite.

"Bon dieu de bon dieu!" howled an injured gentleman. "To sleep is impossible, tas d'imbeciles! - "

And Hélène's window closed with a snap.

Two

The day broke hot and stifling. The first sunbeams which chased the fog from bridge and street also drove the mists from the cool thickets of the Luxembourg Garden, and revealed groups of dragoons picketed in the shrubbery.

"Dragoons in the Luxembourg!" cried the gamins to each other. "What for?"

But even the gamins did not know - yet.

At the great Ateliers of Messieurs Bouguereau and Lefebvre the first day of the week is the busiest - and so, this being Monday, the studios were crowded.

The heat was suffocating. The walls, smeared with the refuse of a hundred palettes, fairly sizzled as they gave off a sickly odor of paint and turpentine. Only two poses had been completed, but the tired models stood or sat, glistening with perspiration. The men drew and painted, many of them stripped to the waist. The air was heavy with tobacco smoke and the respiration of some two hundred students of half as many nationalities.

"Dieu! quel chaleur!" gasped a fat little Frenchman,

mopping his clipped head and breathing hard.

"Clifford," he inquired in English, "ees eet zat you haf a so great - a - heat chez vous?"

Clifford glanced up from his easel. "Heat in New York? My dear Deschamps, this is nothing."

The other eyed him suspiciously.

"You know New York is the capital of Galveston?" said Clifford, slapping on a brush full of color and leaning back to look at it.

The Frenchman didn't know, but he nodded.

"Well, that's very far south. We suffer - yes, we suffer, but our poor poultry suffer more."

"Ze - ze pooltree? Wat eez zat?"

Clifford explained.

"In summer the fire engines are detailed to throw water on the hens to keep their feathers from singeing. Singeing spoils the flavor."

The Frenchman growled.

"One of our national institutions is the `Hen's Mutual Fire Insurance Company,' supported by the Government," added Clifford.

Deschamps snorted.

"That is why," put in Rhodes, lazily dabbing at his

canvas, "why we seldom have omelets - the eggs are so apt to be laid fried."

"How, zen, does eet make ze chicken?" spluttered the Frenchman, his
wrath rising.

"Our chickens are also - " a torrent of bad language from Monsieur Deschamps, and a howl of execration from all the rest, silenced Clifford.

"It's too hot for that sort of thing," pleaded Elliott.

"Idiot!" muttered the Frenchman, shooting ominous glances at the bland youth, who saw nothing.

"C'est l'heure," cried a dozen voices, and the tired model stretched his cramped limbs. Clifford rose, dropped a piece of charcoal down on his neighbor's neck, and stepping across Thaxton's easel, walked over to Gethryn.

"Rex, have you heard the latest?"

"No."

"The Ministry has fallen again, and the Place de la Concorde is filled with people yelling, A bas la Republique! Vive le General Boulanger!"

Gethryn looked serious. Clifford went on, speaking low.

"I saw a troop of cavalry going over this morning, and old Forain told me just now that the regiments at Versailles were ready to move at a minute's notice."

"I suppose things are lively across the river," said Gethryn.

"Exactly, and we're all going over to see the fun. You'll come?"

"Oh, I'll come. Hello! here's Rhodes; tell him."

Rhodes knew. Ministry fallen. Mob at it some more. Been fired on by the soldiers once. Pont Neuf and the Arc guarded by cannon. Carleton came hurrying up.

"The French students are loose and raising Cain. We're going to assist at the show. Come along."

"No," growled Braith, and looked hard at Rex.

"Oh, come along! We're all going," said Carleton, "Elliott, Gethryn, the Colossus, Thaxton, Clifford."

Braith turned sharply to Rex. "Yes, going to get your heads smashed by a bullet or carved by a saber. What for? What business is it of yours?"

"Braith thinks he looks like a Prussian and is afraid," mused Clifford.

"Come on, won't you, Braith?" said Gethryn.

"Are you going?"

"Why not?" said the other, uneasily, "and why won't you?"

"No French mob for me," answered Braith, quietly. "You fellows had better keep away. You don't know what you may get into. I saw the siege, and the man who was in Paris in '71 has seen enough."

"Oh, this is nothing serious," urged Clifford. "If they fire I shall leg it; so will the lordly Reginald; so will we all."

Braith dug his hands into the pockets of his velveteens, and shook his head.

"No," he said, "I've got some work to do. So have you, Rex."

"Come on, we're off," shouted Thaxton from the stairway.

Clifford seized Gethryn's arm, Elliott and Rhodes crowded on behind. A small earthquake shock followed as the crowd of students launched itself down the stairs.

"Braith doesn't approve of my cutting the atelier so often," said Gethryn, "and he's right. I ought to have stayed."

"Reggy going to back out?" cooed Clifford.

"No," said Rex. "Here's Rhodes with a cab."

"It's too hot to walk," gasped Rhodes. "I secured this. It was all I could get. Pile in."

Rex sprang up beside the driver.

"Allons!" he cried, "to the Obelisk!"

"But, monsieur - " expostulated the cabby, "it is today the revolution. I dare not."

"Go on, I tell you," roared Rhodes. "Clifford, take his reins away if he refuses."

Clifford made a snatch at them, but was repulsed by the indignant cabby.

"Go on, do you hear?" shouted the Colossus. The cabman looked at Gethryn.

"Go on!" laughed Rex, "there is no danger."

Jehu lifted his shoulders to the level of his shiny hat, and giving the reins a jerk, muttered, "Crazy English! - Heu - heu - Cocotte!"

In twenty minutes they had arrived at the bridge opposite the Palais Bourbon.

"By Jove!" said Gethryn, "look at that crowd! The Place de la Concorde is black with them!"

The cab stopped with a jolt. Half a dozen policemen stepped into the street. Two seized the horses' heads.

"The bridge is forbidden to vehicles, gentlemen," they said, courteously. "To cross, one must descend."

Clifford began to argue, but Elliott stopped him.

"It's only a step," said he, paying the relieved cabby. "Come ahead!"

In a moment they were across the bridge and pushing

into the crowd, single file.

"What a lot of troops and police!" said Elliott, panting as he elbowed his way through the dense masses. "I tell you, the mob are bent on mischief."

The Place de la Concorde was packed and jammed with struggling, surging humanity. Pushed and crowded up to the second fountain, clinging in bunches to the Obelisk, overrunning the first fountain, and covering the pedestals of the "Cities of France," it heaved, shifted, undulated like clusters of swarming ants.

In the open space about the second fountain was the Prefect of the Seine, surrounded by a staff of officers. He looked worn and anxious as he stood mopping the perspiration from his neck and glancing nervously at his men, who were slowly and gently rolling back the mob. On the bridge a battalion of red-legged soldiers lounged, leaning on their rifles. To the right were long lines of cavalry in shining helmets and cuirasses. The men sat motionless in their saddles, their armor striking white fire in the fierce glow of the midday sun. Ever and anon the faint flutter of a distant bugle announced the approach of more regiments.

Among the shrubbery of the Gardens, a glimmer of orange and blue betrayed the lurking presence of the Guards. Down the endless vistas of the double and quadruple rows of trees stretching out to the Arc, and up the Cour la Reine, long lines of scarlet were moving toward the central point, the Place de la Concorde. The horses of a squadron of hussars pawed and champed across the avenue, the men, in their pale blue jackets, presenting a cool relief to the universal glare. The

Robert W. Chambers

Champs Elysees was deserted, excepting by troops. Not a civilian was to be seen on the bridge. In front of the Madeleine three points of fire blazed and winked in the sun. They were three cannon.

Suddenly, over by the Obelisk, began a hoarse murmur, confused and dull at first, but growing louder, until it swelled into a deafening roar. "Long live Boulanger!" "Down with Ferry!" "Long live the Republic!" As the great wave of sound rose over the crowd and broke sullenly against the somber masses of the Palace of the Bourbons, a thin, shrill cry from the extreme right answered, "Vive la Commune!" Elliott laughed nervously.

"They'll charge those howling Belleville anarchists!"

Clifford began, in pure deviltry, to whistle the Carmagnole.

"Do you want to get us all into hot water?" whispered Thaxton.

"Monsieur is of the Commune?" inquired a little man, suavely.

And, the devil still prompting Clifford, he answered: "Because I whistled the Carmagnole? Bah!"

The man scowled.

"Look here, my friend," said Clifford, "my political principles are yours, and I will be happy to drink at your expense."

The other Americans exchanged looks, and Elliott tried

to check Clifford's folly before it was too late.

"Espion!" muttered the Frenchman, adding, a little louder, "Sale Allemand!"

Gethryn looked up startled.

"Keep cool," whispered Thaxton; "if they think we're Germans we're done for."

Carleton glanced nervously about. "How they stare," he whispered. "Their eyes pop out of their heads as if they saw Bismarck."

There was an ominous movement among the throng.

"Vive l'Anarchie! A bas les Prussiens!" yelled a beetle-browed Italian. "A bas les etrangers!"

"My friend," said Clifford, pleasantly, "you've got a very vile accent yourself."

"You're a Prussian!" screamed the man.

Every one was now looking at them. Gethryn began to fume.

"I'll thrash that cur if he says Prussian again," said he.

"You'll keep quiet, that's what you'll do," growled Thaxton, looking anxiously at Rhodes.

"Yes, you will!" said the Colossus, very pale.

"Pig of a Prussian!" shouted a fearful-looking hag, planting herself in front of Clifford with arms akimbo and head thrust forward. "Pig of a Prussian spy!"

She glanced at her supporters, who promptly applauded.

"Ah - h - h!" she screamed, her little green eyes shining like a tiger's - "Spy! German spy!"

"Madam," said Clifford, politely, "go and wash yourself."

"Hold your cursed tongue, Clifford!" whispered Thaxton. "Do you want to be torn to pieces?"

Suddenly a man behind Gethryn sprang at his back, and then, amazed and terrified at his own daring, yelled lustily for help. Gethryn shook him off as he would a fly, but the last remnant of self-control went at the same time, and, wheeling, he planted a blow square in the fellow's neck. The man fell like an ox. In an instant the mob was upon them. Thaxton received a heavy kick in the ribs, which sent him reeling against Carleton. Clifford knocked two men down in as many blows, and, springing back, stood guard over Thaxton until he could struggle to his feet again. Elliott got a sounding thwack on the nose, which he neatly returned, adding one on the eye for interest. Gethryn and Carleton fought back to back. Rhodes began by half strangling a son of the Commune and then flung him bodily among his howling compatriots.

"Good Heavens," gasped Rhodes, "we can't keep this up!" And raising his voice, he cried with all the force of his lungs, "Help! This way, police!" A shot answered him, and a man, clapping his hands to his face, tilted heavily forward, the blood spurting between his fingers.

Then a terrible cry arose, a din in which the Americans caught the clanging of steel and the neighing of horses. A man was hurled violently against Gethryn, who, losing in turn his balance, staggered and fell. Rising to his knees, he saw a great foam-covered horse rearing almost over him, and a red-faced rider in steel helmet and tossing plume slashing furiously among the crowd. Next moment he was dragged to his feet and back into the flying mob.

"Look out," panted Thaxton, "the cavalry - they've charged - run!" Gethryn glanced over his shoulder. All along the edge of the frantic, panic-stricken crowd the gleaming crests of the cavalry surged and dashed like a huge wave of steel.

Cries, groans, and curses rose and were drowned in the thunder of the charging horses and the clashing of weapons.

"Spy!" screamed a voice in his ear. Gethryn turned, but the fellow was legging it for safety.

Suddenly he saw a woman who, pushed and crowded by the mob, stumbled and fell. In a moment he was by her side, bent over to raise her, was hurled upon his face, rose blinded by dust and half-stunned, but dragging her to her feet with him.

Swept onward by the rush, knocked this way and that, he still managed to support the dazed woman, and by degrees succeeded in controlling his own course, which he bent toward the Obelisk. As he neared the goal of comparative safety, exhausted, he suffered himself and the woman to be carried on by the rush. Then a blinding flash split the air in front, and the crash of musketry almost in his face hurled him back.

Men threw up their hands and sank in a heap or spun round and pitched headlong. For a moment he swayed in the drifting smoke. A blast of hot, sickening air enveloped him. Then a dull red cloud seemed to settle slowly, crushing, grinding him into the earth.

Three

When Gethryn unclosed his eyes the dazzling sunlight almost blinded him. A thousand grotesque figures danced before him, a hot red vapor seemed to envelop him. He felt a dull pain in his ears and a numb sensation about the legs. Gradually he recalled the scene that had just passed; the flying crowd lashed by that pitiless iron scourge; the cruel panic; the mad, suffocating rush; and then that crash of thunder which had crushed him.

He lay quite still, not offering to move. A strange languor seemed to weigh down his very heart. The air reeked with powder smoke. Not a breath was stirring.

Presently the numbness in his knees changed to a hot, pricking throb. He tried to move his legs, but found he could not. Then a sudden thought sent the blood with a rush to his heart. Perhaps he no longer had any legs! He remembered to have heard of legless men whose phantom members caused them many uncomfortable sensations. He certainly had a dull pain where his legs belonged, but the question was, had he legs also? The doubt was too much, and with a faint cry he struggled to rise.

"The devil!" exclaimed a voice close to his head, and a

Robert W. Chambers

pair of startled eyes met his own. " The devil!" repeated the owner of the eyes, as if to a apostrophize some particular one. He was a bird-like little fellow, with thin canary-colored hair and eyebrows and colorless eyes, and he was seated upon a campstool about two feet from Gethryn's head.

He blinked at Gethryn. "These Frenchmen," said he, "have as many lives as a cat."

"Thanks!" said Gethryn, smiling faintly.

"An Englishman! The devil!" shouted the pale-eyed man, hopping in haste from his campstool and dropping a well-thumbed sketching-block as he did so.

"Don't be an ass," suggested Gethryn; "you'd much better help me to get up."

"Look here," cried the other, "how was I to know you were not done for?"

"What's the matter with me?" said Gethryn. "Are my - my legs gone?"

The little man glanced at Gethryn's shoes.

No, they're all there, unless you originally had more than the normal number - in fact I'm afraid - I think you're all right.

Gethryn stared at him.

"And what the devil am I to do with this sketch?" he continued, kicking the fallen block. "I've been at it for an hour. It isn't half bad, you know. I was going to call it `Love in Death.' It was for the London Illustrated Mirror."

Gethryn lay quite still. He had decided the little fellow was mad.

"Dead in each other's arms!" continued the stranger, sentimentally. "She so fair - he so brave - "

Gethryn sprang up impatiently, but only a little way. Something held him down and he fell back.

"Do you want to get up?" asked the stranger.

"I should rather think so."

The other bent down and placed his hands under Gethryn's arms, and - half helped, half by his own impatient efforts - Rex sat up, leaning against the other man. A sharp twinge shot through the numbness of his legs, and his eyes, seeking the cause, fell upon the body of a woman. She lay across his knees, apparently dead. Rex remembered her now for the first time.

"Lift her," he said weakly.

The little man with some difficulty succeeded in moving the body; then Gethryn, putting one arm around the other's neck, struggled up. He was stiff, and toppled about a little, but before long he was pretty steady on his feet.

"The woman," he said, "perhaps she is not dead."

"Dead she is," said the Artist of the Mirror cheerfully, gathering up his pencils, which lay scattered on the steps of the pedestal. He leaned over the little heap of crumpled clothing.

"Shot, I fancy," he muttered.

Gethryn, feeling his strength returning and the circulation restored to his limbs, went over to the place where she lay.

"Have you a flask?" he asked. The little Artist eyed him suspiciously.

"Are you a newspaperman?"

"No, an art student."

"Nothing to do with newspapers?"

"No."

"I don't drink," said the queer little person.

"I never said you did," said Gethryn. "Have you a flask, or haven't you?"

The stranger slowly produced one, and poured a few drops into his pink palm.

"We may as well try," he said, and began to chafe her forehead. "Here, take the whiskey - let it trickle, so, between her teeth. Don't spill any more than you can help," he added.

"Has she been shot?" asked Gethryn.

"Crushed, maybe."

"Poor little thing, look at her roll of music!" said Gethryn, wiping a few drops of blood from her pallid face, and glancing compassionately at the helpless, dust-covered figure.

"I'm afraid it's no use - "

"Give her some more whiskey, quick!" interrupted the stranger.

Gethryn tremblingly poured a few more drops between the parted lips. A faint color came into her temples. She moved, shivered from head to foot, and then, with a half-choked sob, opened her eyes.

"Mon Dieu, comme je souffre!"

"Where do you suffer?" said Gethryn gently.

"The arm; I think it is broken."

Gethryn stood up and looked about for help. The Place was nearly deserted. The blue-jacketed hussars were still standing over by the Avenue, and an occasional heavy, red-faced cuirassier walked his sweating horse slowly up and down the square. A few policemen lounged against the river wall, chatting with the sentries, and far down the dusty Rue Royale, the cannon winked and blinked before the Church of the Madeleine.

The rumble of wheels caused him to turn. A clumsy, blue-covered wagon drew up at the second fountain. It was a military ambulance. A red-capped trooper sprang down jingling from one of the horses, and was joined by two others who had followed the ambulance and who also dismounted. Then the three approached a group of policemen who were lifting something from the pavement. At the same moment he heard voices beside him, and turning, found that the girl had risen and was sitting on the campstool, her head leaning against the little stranger's shoulder.

An officer stood looking down at her. His boots were spotless. The band of purple on his red and gold cap showed that he was a surgeon.

"Can we be of any assistance to madame?" he inquired.

"I was looking for a cab," said Gethryn, "but perhaps she is not strong enough to be taken to her home."

A frightened look came into the girl's face and she glanced anxiously at the ambulance. The surgeon knelt quietly beside her.

"Madame is not seriously hurt," he said, after a rapid examination. "The right arm is a little strained, but it will be nothing, I assure you, Madame; a matter of a few days, that is all."

He rose and stood brushing the knees of his trousers with his handkerchief. "Monsieur is a foreigner?"

Gethryn smiled. "The accent?"

"On the contrary, I assure you, Monsieur," cried the officer with more politeness than truth. He eyed the ambulance. "The people of Paris have learned a lesson today," he said.

A trooper clattered up, leading an officer's horse, and

dismounted, saluting. The young surgeon glanced at his watch.

"Picard," he said, "stop a closed cab and send it here."

The trooper wheeled his horse and galloped away across the square, and the officer turned to the others.

"Madame, I trust, will soon recover," he said courteously. "Madame, messieurs, I have the honor to salute you." And with many a clink and jingle, he sprang into the saddle and clattered away in the wake of the slowly moving ambulance.

At the corner of the Rue Royale, Gethryn saw the trooper stop a cab and point to the Obelisk. He went over and asked the canary-colored stranger, "Will you take her home, or shall I?"

"Why, you, of course; you brought her here."

"No, I didn't. I never saw her until I noticed her being pushed about by the crowd." He caught the girl's eye and colored furiously, hoping she did not suspect the nature of their discussion. Before her helplessness it seemed so brutal.

The cab drew up before the Obelisk and a gruff voice cried, "V'la! M'ssieurs! - 'dames!"

"Put your arm on my shoulder - so," said Gethryn, and the two men raised her gently. Once in the cab, she sank back, looking limp and white. Gethryn turned sharply to the other man.

"Shall I go?"

"Rather," replied the little stranger, pleasantly.

Opening his coat in haste, he produced a square of pasteboard. "My card," he said, offering one to Gethryn, who bowed and fumbled in his pockets. As usual, his card-case was in another coat.

"I'm sorry I have none," he said at length, "but my name is Reginald Gethryn, and I shall give myself the pleasure of calling to thank you for - "

"For nothing," laughed the other, "excepting for the sketch, which you may have when you come to see me."

"Thanks, and au revoir," glancing at the card. "Au revoir, Mr Bulfinch."

He was giving the signal to the cabby when his new acquaintance stopped him.

"You're quite sure - you - er - don't know any newspapermen?"

"Quite."

"All right - all right - and - er - just don't mention about my having a flask, if you do meet any of them. I - er - keep it for others. I don't drink."

"Certainly not," began Gethryn, but Mr T. Hoppley Bulfinch had seized his campstool and trotted away across the square.

Gethryn leaned into the cab.

"Will you give me your address?" he asked gently.

"Rue Monsieur le Prince - 430 - " she whispered. "Do you know where it is?"

"Yes," said Gethryn. It was his own number.

"Rue Monsieur le Prince 430", he repeated to the driver, and stepping in, softly shut the door.

Four

Rain was falling steadily. The sparrows huddled under the eaves, or hopped disconsolately along the window-sills, uttering short, ill-tempered chirps. The wind was rising, blowing in quick, sharp gusts and sweeping the forest of rain spears, rank upon rank, in mad dashes against the glass-roofed studio.

Gethryn, curled up in a corner of his sofa, listlessly watched the showers of pink and white blossoms which whirled and eddied down from the rocking chestnuts, falling into the windy court in little heaps. One or two stiff-legged flies crawled rheumatically along the window glass, only to fall on their backs and lie there buzzing.

The two bull pups had silently watched the antics of these maudlin creatures, but their interest changed to indignation when one sodden insect attempted a final ascent and fell noisily upon the floor under their very noses. Then they rose as one dog and leaped madly upon the intruder, or meant to; but being pups, and uncertain in their estimation of distances, they brought up with startled yelps against the wall. Gethryn took them in his arms, where they found consolation in chewing the buttons off his coat. The parrot had driven the raven nearly crazy by turning upside down and staring at him for fifteen minutes of insulting silence. Mrs Gummidge was engaged in a matronly and sedate toilet, interrupting herself now and then to bestow a critical glance upon the parrot. She heartily approved of his attitude toward the raven, and although the old cynic cared nothing for Mrs Gummidge's opinion, he found a sour satisfaction in warning her of her enemy's hostile intentions. This he always did with a croak, causing Mrs Gummidge to look up just in time, and the raven to hop back disconcerted.

The rain beat a constant tattoo on the roof, and this, mingling with the drowsy purr of the cat, who was now marching to and fro with tail erect in front of Gethryn, exercised a soothing influence, and presently a snore so shocked the parrot that he felt obliged to relieve his mind by a series of intricate gymnastics upon his perch.

Gethryn was roused by a violent hammering on his door. The room had grown dark, and night had come on while he slept.

"All right - coming," he shouted, groping his way across the room. Slipping the bolt, he opened the door and looked out, but could see nothing in the dark hallway. Then he felt himself seized and hugged and dragged back into his studio, where he was treated to a heavy slap on the shoulder. Then someone struck a match and presently, by the light of a candle, he saw Clifford and Elliott, and farther back in the shade another form which he thought he knew.

Clifford began, "Here you are! We thought you were dead - killed through my infernal fooling." He turned very red, and stammered, "Tell him, Elliott."

"Why, you see," said Elliott, "we've been hunting for you high and low since the fight yesterday afternoon. Clifford was nearly crazy. He said it was his fault. We went to the Morgue and then to the hospitals, and finally to the police - " A knock interrupted him, and a policeman appeared at the door.

Clifford looked sheepish.

"The young gentleman who is missing - this is his room?" inquired the policeman.

"Oh, he's found - he's all right," said Clifford, hurriedly. The officer stared.

"Here he is," said Elliott, pointing to Rex.

The man transferred his stare to Gethryn, but did not offer to move.

"I am the supposed deceased," laughed Rex, with a little bow.

"But how am I to know?" said the officer.

"Why, here I am."

"But," said the man, suspiciously, "I want to know how I am to know?"

"Nonsense," said Elliott, laughing.

"But, Monsieur," expostulated the officer, politely.

"This is Reginald Gethryn, artist, I tell you!"

The policeman shrugged his shoulders. He was noncommittal and very polite.

"Messieurs," he said, "my orders are to lock up this room."

"But it's my room, I can't spare my room," laughed Gethryn. "From whom did you take your orders?"

"From Monsieur the Prefect of the Seine."

"Oh, it is all right, then," said Gethryn. "Take a seat."

He went to his desk, wrote a hasty note, and then called the man. "Read that, if you please, Monsieur Sergeant de Ville."

The man's eyes grew round. "Certainly, Monsieur, I will take the note to the Prefect," he said; "Monsieur will pardon the intrusion."

"Don't mention it," said Rex, smiling, and slipped a franc into his big red fist. The officer pocketed it with a demure "Merci, Monsieur," and presently the clank of his bayonet died away on the stairs.

"Well," said Elliott, "you're found." Clifford was beginning again with self-reproaches and self-abasement, but Rex broke in: "You fellows are awfully good - I do assure you I appreciate it. But I wasn't in any more danger than the rest of you. What about Thaxton and the Colossus and Carleton?" He grew anxious as he named them.

"We all got off with no trouble at all, only we missed you - and then the troops fired, and they chased us over

Robert W. Chambers

the bridge and scattered us in the Quarter, and we all drifted one by one into the Café des Écoles. And then you didn't come, and we waited till after dinner, and finally came here to find your door locked - "

"Oh!" burst out Clifford, "I tell you, Rex - damn it! I will express my feelings!"

"No, you won't," said Rex; "drop 'em, old boy, don't express 'em. Here we are - that's enough, isn't it, Shakespeare?"

The bird had climbed to Gethryn's shoulder and was cocking his eye fondly at Clifford. They were dear friends. Once he had walked up Clifford's arm and had grabbed him by the ear, for which Clifford, more in sorrow than in anger, soaked him in cold water. Since that, their mutual understanding had been perfect.

"Where are you going to, you old fiend?" said Clifford, tickling the parrot's throat.

"Hell!" shrieked the bird.

"Good Heavens! I never taught him that," said Gethryn.

Clifford smiled, without committing himself.

"But where were you, Rex?" asked Elliott.

Rex flushed. "Hullo," cried Clifford, "here's Reginald blushing. If I didn't know him better I'd swear there's a woman in it." The dark figure at the end of the room rose and walked swiftly over, and Rex saw that it was Braith, as he had supposed.

"I swear I forgot him," laughed Elliott. "What a queer bird you are, Braith, squatting over there as silent as a stuffed owl!"

"He has been walking his legs off after you," began Clifford, but Braith cut him short with a brusque -

"Where were you, Rex?"

Gethryn winced. "I'd rather - I think" - he began, slowly -

"Excuse me - it's not my business," growled Braith, throwing himself into a seat and beginning to rub Mrs Gummidge the wrong way. "Confound the cat!" he added, examining some red parallel lines which suddenly decorated the back of his hand.

"She won't stand rubbing the wrong way," said Rex, smiling uneasily.

"Like the rest of us," said Elliott.

"More fool he who tries it," said Braith, and looked at Gethryn with an affectionate smile that made him turn redder than before.

"Rex," began Clifford again, with that fine tact for which he was celebrated, "own up! You spent last night warbling under the windows of Lisette."

"Or Frisette," said Elliott, "or Cosette."

"Or Babette, Lisette, Frisette, Cosette, Babette!" chanted the two young men in a sort of catch.

Braith so seldom swore, that the round oath with which he broke into their vocal exercises stopped them through sheer astonishment. But Clifford, determined on self-assertion and loving an argument, especially out of season, turned on Braith and began:

"Why should not Youth love?"

"Love! Bah!" said Braith.

"Why Bah?" he persisted, stimulated by the disgust of Braith. "Now if a man - take Elliott, for example - "

"Take yourself," cried the other.

"Well - myself, for example. Suppose when my hours of weary toil are over - returning to my lonely cell, I encounter the blue eyes of Ninette on the way, or the brown eyes of Cosette, or perhaps the black eyes of - "

Braith stamped impatiently.

"Lisette," said Clifford, sweetly. "Why should I not refresh my drooping spirits by adoring Lisette - Cos- "

"Oh, come, you said that before," said Gethryn. "You're getting to be a bore, Clifford."

"You at least can no longer reproach me," said the other, with a quick look that increased Gethryn's embarrassment.

"Let him talk his talk of bewitching grisettes, and gay students," said Braith, more angry than Rex had ever seen him. "He's never content except when he's dangling after some fool worse than himself. Damn this `Bohemian love' rot! I've been here longer than you have, Clifford," he said, suddenly softening and turning half apologetically to the latter, who nodded to intimate that he hadn't taken offense. "I've seen all that shabby romance turn into such reality as you wouldn't like to face. I've seen promising lives go out in ruin and disgrace - here in this very street - in this very house - lives that started exactly on the lines that you are finding so mighty pleasant just now."

Clifford was in danger of being silenced. That would never do.

"Papa Braith," he smiled, "is it that you too have been through the mill? Shall I present your compliments to the miller? I'm going. Come, Elliott."

Elliott took up his hat and followed.

"Braith," he said, "we'll drink your health as we go through the mill."

"Remember that the mill grinds slowly but surely," said Braith.

"He speaks in parables," laughed Clifford, halfway downstairs, and the two took up the catch they had improvised, singing, "Lisette - Cosette - Ninette - " in thirds more or less out of tune, until Gethryn shut the door on the last echoes that came up from the hall below.

Gethryn came back and sat down, and Braith took a seat beside him, but neither spoke. Braith had his pipe and Rex his cigarette.

When the former was ready, he began to speak. He could not conceal the effort it cost him, but that wore away after he had been talking a while.

"Rex," he began, "when I say that we are friends, I mean, for my own part, that you are more to me than any man alive; and now I am going to tell you my story. Don't interrupt me. I have only just courage enough; if any of it oozes out, I may not be able to go on. Well, I have been through the mill. Clifford was right. They say it is a phase through which all men must pass. I say, must or not, if you pass through it you don't come out without a stain. You're never the same man after. Don't imagine I mean that I was brutally dissolute. I don't want you to think worse of me than I deserve. I kept a clean tongue in my head - always. So do you. I never got drunk - neither do you. I kept a distance between myself and the women whom those fellows were celebrating in song just now - so do you. How much is due in both of us to principle, and how much to fastidiousness, Rex? I found out for myself at last, and perhaps your turn will not be long in coming. After avoiding entanglements for just three years - " He looked at Rex, who dropped his head - "I gave in to a temptation as coarse, vulgar and silly as any I had ever despised. Why? Heaven knows. She was as vulgar a leech as ever fastened on a calf like myself. But I didn't think so then. I was wildly in love with her. She said she was madly in love with me." Braith made a grimace of such disgust that Rex would have laughed, only he saw in time that it was self-disgust which made Braith's mouth look so set and hard.

"I wanted to marry her. She wouldn't marry me. I was not rich, but what she said was: `One hates one's husband.' When I say vulgar, I don't mean she had vulgar manners. She was as pretty and trim and clever - as the rest of them. An artist, if he sees all that really exists, sometimes also sees things which have no existence at all. Of these were the qualities with which I invested her - the moral and mental correspondencies to her blonde skin and supple figure. She justified my perspicacity one day by leaving me for a loathsome little Jew. The last time I heard of her she had been turned out of a gambling hell in his company. His name is Emanuel Pick. Is not this a shabby romance? Is it not enough to make a self-respecting man hang his head - to know that he has once found pleasure in the society of the mistress of Mr Emanuel Pick?"

A long silence followed, during which the two men smoked, looking in opposite directions. At last Braith reached over and shook the ashes out of his pipe. Rex lighted a fresh cigarette at the same time, and their eyes met with a look of mutual confidence and goodwill. Braith spoke again, firmly this time.

"God keep you out of the mire, Rex; you're all right thus far. But it is my solemn belief that an affair of that kind would be your ruin as an artist; as a man."

"The Quarter doesn't regard things in that light," said Gethryn, trying hard to laugh off the weight that oppressed him.

"The Quarter is a law unto itself. Be a law unto yourself, Rex - Good night, old chap."

"Good night, Braith," said Gethryn slowly.

Five

Thirion's at six pm. Madame Thirion, neat and demure, sat behind her desk; her husband, in white linen apron and cap, scuttled back and forth shouting, "Bon! Bon!" to the orders that came down the call trumpet. The waiters flew crazily about, and cries went up for "Pierre" and "Jean" and "green peas and fillet."

The noise, smoke, laughter, shouting, rattle of dishes, the penetrating odor of burnt paper and French tobacco, all proclaimed the place a Latin Quarter restaurant. The English and Americans ate like civilized beings and howled like barbarians. The Germans, when they had napkins, tucked them under their chins. The Frenchmen - well! they often agreed with the hated Teuton in at least one thing; that knives were made to eat with. But which of the four nationalities exceeded the others in turbulence and bad language would be hard to say.

Clifford was eating his chop and staring at the blonde adjunct of a dapper little Frenchman.

"Clifford," said Carleton, "stop that."

"I'm mesmerizing her," said Clifford. "It's a case of hypnotism."

The girl, who had been staring back at Clifford, suddenly shrugged her shoulders, and turning to her companion, said aloud:

"How like a monkey, that foreigner!"

Clifford withdrew his eyes in a hurry, amid a roar of laughter from the others. He was glad when Braith's entrance caused a diversion.

"Hullo, Don Juan! I see you, Lothario! Drinking again?"

Braith took it all as a matter of course, but this time failed to return as good as they gave. He took a seat beside Gethryn and said in a low tone:

"I've just come from your house. There's a letter from the Salon in your box."

Gethryn set down his wine untasted and reached for his hat.

"What's the matter, Reggy? Has Lisette gone back on you?" asked Clifford, tenderly.

"It's the Salon," said Braith, as Gethryn went out with a hasty "Good night."

"Poor Reggy, how hard he takes it!" sighed Clifford.

Gethryn hurried along the familiar streets with his heart in his boots sometimes, and sometimes in his mouth.

In his box was a letter and a note addressed in pencil.

He snatched them both, and lighting a candle, mounted the stairs, unlocked his door and sank breathless upon the lounge. He tore open the first envelope. A bit of paper fell out. It was from Braith and said:

I congratulate you either way. If you are successful I shall be as glad as you are. If not, I still congratulate you on the manly courage which you are going to show in turning defeat into victory.

"He's one in a million," thought Gethryn, and opened the other letter. It contained a folded paper and a card. The card was white. The paper read:

You are admitted to the Salon with a No. 1. My compliments. J. Lefebvre

He ought to have been pleased, but instead he felt weak and giddy, and the pleasure was more like pain. He leaned against the table quite unstrung, his mind in a whirl. He got up and went to the window. Then he shook himself and walked over to his cabinet. Taking out a bunch of keys, he selected one and opened what Clifford called his "cellar."

Clifford knew and deplored the fact that Gethryn's "cellar" was no longer open to the public. Since the day when Rex returned from Julien's, tired and cross, to find a row of empty bottles on the floor and Clifford on the sofa conversing incoherently with himself, and had his questions interrupted by a maudlin squawk from the parrot - also tipsy - since that day Gethryn had carried the key. He now produced a wine glass and a dusty bottle, filled the one from the other and emptied it three times in rapid succession. Then he took the glass to the washbasin and rinsed it with great slowness and precision. Then he sat down and tried to think. Number One meant a mention, perhaps a medal. He would telegraph his aunt tomorrow. Suddenly he felt a strong desire to tell someone. He would go and see Braith. No, Braith was in the evening class at the Beaux Arts; so were the others, excepting Clifford and Elliott, and they were at a ball across the river.

Whom could he see? He thought of the garçon. He would ring him up and give him a glass of wine. Alcide was a good fellow and stole very little. The clock struck eleven.

"No, he's gone to bed. Alcide, you've missed a glass of wine and a cigar, you early bird."

His head was clear enough now. He realized his good fortune. He had never been so happy in his life. He called the pups and romped with them until an unlucky misstep sent Mrs Gummidge, with a shriek, to the top of the wardrobe, whence she glared at Gethryn and spit at the delighted raven.

The young man sat down fairly out of breath, but the pups still kept making charges at his legs and tumbled over themselves with barking. He gathered them up and carried them into his bedroom to their sleeping box. As he stooped to drop them in, there came a knock at his studio door. But when he hastened to open it, glad of company, there was no one there. Surprised, he turned back and saw on the floor before him a note. Picking it up, he took it to the lamp and read it. It was signed, "Yvonne Descartes."

When he had read it twice, he sat down to think. Presently he took something out of his waistcoat pocket and held it close to the light. It was a gold brooch in the shape of a fleur-de-lis. On the back was engraved "Yvonne." He held it in his hand a while, and then, getting up, went slowly towards the door. He opened the door, closed it behind him and moved toward the stairs. Suddenly he started.

"Braith! Is that you?"

There was no answer. His voice sounded hollow in the tiled hallway.

"Braith," he said again. "I thought I heard him say `Rex.'" But he kept on to the next floor and stopped before the door of the room which was directly under his own. He paused, hesitated, looking up at a ray of light which came out from a crack in the transom.

"It's too late," he muttered, and turned away irresolutely.

A clear voice called from within, "Entrez donc, Monsieur."

He opened the door and went in.

On a piano stood a shaded lamp, which threw a soft yellow light over everything. The first glance gave him a hasty impression of a white lace-covered bed and a dainty toilet table on which stood a pair of tall silver candlesticks; and then, as the soft voice spoke again, "Will Monsieur be seated?" he turned and confronted the girl whom he had helped in the Place de la Concorde. She lay in a cloud of fleecy wrappings on a lounge that was covered with a great white bearskin. Her blue eyes met Gethryn's, and he smiled faintly.

She spoke again:

"Will Monsieur sit a little nearer? It is difficult to speak loudly - I have so little strength."

Gethryn walked over to the sofa and half unconsciously sank down on the rug which fell on the floor by the invalid's side. He spoke as he would to a sick child.

"I am so very glad you are better. I inquired of the concierge and she told me."

A slight color crept into the girl's face. "You are so good. Ah! what should I have done - what can I say?" She stopped; there were tears in her eyes.

"Please say nothing - please forget it."

"Forget!" Presently she continued, almost in a whisper, "I had so much to say to you, and now you are really here, I can think of nothing, only that you saved me."

"Mademoiselle - I beg!"

She lay silent a moment more; then she raised herself from the sofa and held out her hand. His hand and eyes met hers.

"I thank you," she said, "I can never forget." Then she sank back among the white fluff of lace and fur. "I only learned this morning," she went on, after a minute, " who sat beside me all that night and bathed my arm, and gave me cooling drinks."

Gethryn colored. "There was no one else to take care

of you. I sent for my friend, Doctor Ducrot, but he was out of town. Then Dr Bouvier promised to come, and didn't. The concierge was ill herself - I could not leave you alone. You know, you were a little out of your head with fright and fever. I really couldn't leave you to get on by yourself."

"No," cried the girl, excitedly, "you could not leave me after carrying me out of that terrible crowd; yourself hurt, exhausted, you sat by my side all night long."

Gethryn laid his hand on her. "Hélène," he said, half jesting, "I did what anyone else would have done under the circumstances - and forgotten."

She looked at him shyly. "Don't forget," she said.

"I couldn't forget your face," he rashly answered, moved by the emotion she showed.

She brightened.

"Did you know me when you first saw me in the crowd?" She expected him to say "Yes."

"No," he replied, "I only saw you were a woman and in danger of your life."

The brightness fell from her face. "Then it was all the same to you who I was."

He nodded. "Yes - any woman, you know."

"Old and dirty and ugly?"

His hand slipped from hers. "And a woman - yes."

She shrugged her pretty shoulders. "Then I wish it had been someone else."

"So do I, for your sake," he answered gravely.

She glanced at him, half frightened; then leaning swiftly toward him:

"Forgive me; I would not change places with a queen."

"Nor I with any man!" he cried gayly. "Am I not Paris?"

"And I?"

"You are Hélène," he said, laughing. "Let me see - Paris and Hélène would not have changed - "

She interrupted him impatiently. "Words! you do not mean them. Nor do I, either," she added, hastily. After that neither spoke for a while. Gethryn, half stretched on the big rug, idly twisting bits of it into curls, felt very comfortable, without troubling to ask himself what would come next. Presently she glanced up.

"Paris, do you want to smoke?"

"You don't think I would smoke in this dainty nest?"

"Please do, I like it. We are - we will be such very good friends. There are matches on that table in the silver box."

He shook his head, laughing. "You are too indulgent."

"I am never indulgent, excepting to myself. But I have

caprices and I generally die when they are not indulged. This is one. Please smoke."

"Oh, in that case, with Hélène's permission."

She laughed delightedly as he blew the rings of fragrant smoke far up to the ceiling. There was another long pause, then she began again:

"Paris, you speak French very well."

He came from where he had been standing by the table and seated himself once more among the furs at her feet.

"Do I, Hélène?"

"Yes - but you sing it divinely."

Gethryn began to hum the air of the dream song, smiling, "Yes 'tis a dream - a dream of love," he repeated, but stopped.

Yvonne's temples and throat were crimson.

"Please open the window," she cried, "it's so warm here."

"Hélène, I think you are blushing," said he, mischievously.

She turned her head away from him. He rose and opened the window, leaning out a moment; his heart was beating violently. Presently he returned.

"It's one o'clock."

No answer.

"Hélène, it's one o'clock in the morning."

"Are you tired?" she murmured.

"No."

"Nor I - don't go."

"But it's one o'clock."

"Don't go yet."

He sank down irresolutely on the rug again. "I ought to go," he murmured.

"Are we to remain friends?"

"That is for Hélène to say."

"And Hélène will leave it to Homer!"

"To whom?" said Gethryn.

"Monsieur Homer," said the girl, faintly.

"But that was a tragedy."

"But they were friends."

"In a way. Yes, in a way."

Gethryn tried to return to a light tone. "They fell in love, I believe." No answer. "Very well," said Gethryn, still trying to joke, "I will carry you off in a boat, then."

"To Troy - when?"

"No, to Meudon, when you are well. Do you like the country?"

"I love it," she said.

"Well, I'll take my easel and my paints along too."

She looked at him seriously. "You are an artist - I heard that from the concierge."

"Yes," said Gethryn, "I think I may claim the title tonight."

And then he told her about the Salon. She listened and brightened with sympathy. Then she grew silent.

"Do you paint landscapes?"

"Figures," said the young man, shortly.

"From models?"

"Of course," he answered, still more drily.

"Draped," she persisted.

"No."

"I hate models!" she cried out, almost fiercely.

"They are not a pleasing set, as a rule," he admitted. "But I know some decent ones."

She shivered and shook her curly head. "Some are very pretty, I suppose."

"Some."

"Do you know Sarah Brown?"

"Yes, I know Sarah."

"Men go wild about her."

"I never did."

Yvonne was out of humor. "Oh," she cried, petulantly, "you are very cold - you Americans - like ice."

"Because we don't run after Sarah?"

"Because you are a nation of business, and - "

"And brains," said Gethryn, drily.

There was an uncomfortable pause. Gethryn looked at the girl. She lay with her face turned from him.

"Hélène!" No answer. "Yvonne - Mademoiselle!" No answer. "It's two o'clock."

A slight impatient movement of the head.

"Good night." Gethryn rose. "Good night," he repeated. He waited for a moment. "Good night, Yvonne," he said, for the third time.

She turned slowly toward him, and as he looked down at her he felt a tenderness as for a sick child.

Robert W. Chambers

"Good night," he said once more, and, bending over her, gently laid the little gold clasp in her open hand. She looked at it in surprise; then suddenly she leaned swiftly toward him, rested a brief second against him, and then sank back again. The golden fleur-de-lis glittered over his heart.

"You will wear it?" she whispered.

"Yes."

"Then - good night."

Half unconsciously he stooped and kissed her forehead; then went his way. And all that night one slept until the morning broke, and one saw morning break, then fell asleep.

Six

It was the first day of June. In the Luxembourg Gardens a soft breeze stirred the tender chestnut leaves, and blew sparkling ripples across the water in the Fountain of Marie de Medicis.

The modest little hothouse flowers had quite recovered from the shock of recent transplanting and were ambitiously pushing out long spikes and clusters of crimson, purple and gold, filling the air with spicy perfume, and drawing an occasional battered butterfly, gaunt and seedy, from his long winter's sleep, but still remembering the flowery days of last season's brilliant debut.

Through the fresh young leaves the sunshine fell, dappling the glades and thickets, bathing the gray walls of the Palais du Sénat, and almost warming into life the queer old statues of long departed royalty, which for so many years have looked down from the great terrace to the Palace of the King.

Through every gate the people drifted into the gardens, and the winding paths were dotted and crowded with brightly-colored, slowly-moving groups.

Here a half dozen meager, black-robed priests strolled

silently amid the tender verdure; here a noisy crowd of children, gamboling awkwardly in the wake of a painted rubber ball, made day hideous with their yells.

Now a slovenly company of dragoons shuffled by, their big shapeless boots covered with dust, and their whalebone plumes hanging in straight points to the middle of their backs; now a group of strutting students and cocottes passed noisily, the girls in spotless spring plumage, the students vying with each other in the display of blinking eyeglasses, huge bunchy neckties, and sleek checked trousers. Policemen, trim little grisettes (for whatever is said to the contrary, the grisette is still extant in Paris), nurse girls with turbaned heads and ugly red streamers, wheeling ugly red babies; an occasional stray zouave or turco in curt Turkish jacket and white leggings; grave old gentlemen with white mustache and military step; gay, baggy gentlemen from St Cyr, looking like newly-painted wooden soldiers; students from the Ecole Polytechnique; students from the Lycée St Louis in blue and red; students from Julien's and the Beaux Arts with a plentiful sprinkling of berets and corduroy jackets; and group after group of jingling artillery officers in scarlet and black, or hussars and chasseurs in pale turquoise, strolled and idled up and down the terrace, or watched the toy yachts braving the furies of the great fountain.

Over by the playgrounds, the Polichinel nuisance drummed and squeaked to an appreciative audience of tender years. The "Jeu de paume" was also in full swing, a truly exasperating spectacle for a modern tennis player.

The old man who feeds the sparrows in the afternoon,

and beats his wife at night, was intent on the former cheerful occupation, and smiled benevolently upon the little children who watched him, open mouthed. The numerous waterfowl - mallard, teal, red-head, and dusky - waddled and dived and fought the big mouse-colored pigeons for a share of the sparrow's crumbs.

A depraved and mongrel pointer, who had tugged at his chain in a wild endeavor to point the whole heterogeneous mass of feathered creatures from sparrow to swan, lost his head and howled dismally until dragged off by the lean-legged student who was attached to the other end of the chain.

Gethryn, sprawling on a bench in the sunshine, turned up his nose. Braith grunted scornfully.

A man passed in the crowd, stopped, stared, and then hastily advanced toward Gethryn.

"You?" said Rex, smiling and shaking hands. "Mr Clifford, this is Mr Bulfinch; Mr Braith," - but Mr Bulfinch was already bowing to Braith and offering his hand, though with a curious diminution of his first beaming cordiality. Braith's constraint was even more marked. He had turned quite white. Bulfinch and Gethryn, who had risen to receive him, remained standing side by side, stranded on the shoals of an awkward situation. The little Mirror man made a grab at a topic which he thought would float them off, and laid hold instead on one which upset them altogether.

"I hope Mrs Braith is well. She met you all right at Vienna?"

Braith bowed stiffly, without answering.

Rex gave him a quick look, and turning on his heel, said carelessly:

"I see you and Mr Braith are old acquaintances, so I won't scruple to leave you with him for a moment. Bring Mr Bulfinch over to the music stand, Braith." And smiling, as if he were assisting at a charming reunion, he led Clifford away. The latter turned, as he departed, an eye of delighted intelligence upon Braith.

To renew his acquaintance with Mr Bulfinch was the last thing Braith desired, but since the meeting had been thrust upon him he thanked Gethryn's tact for removing such a witness of it as Clifford would have been. He had no intention, however, of talking with the little Mirror man, and maintained a profound silence, smoking steadily. This conduct so irritated the other that he determined to force an explanation of the matter which seemed so distasteful to his ungracious companion. He certainly thought he had his own reasons for resenting the sight of Braith upon a high horse, and he resumed the conversation with all the jaunty ease which the calling of newspaper correspondent is said to cultivate.

"I hope Mrs Braith found no difficulty in meeting you in Vienna?"

"Madame was not my wife, and we did not meet in Vienna," said Braith shortly.

Bulfinch began to stare, and to feel a little less at ease.

"She told me - that is, her courier came to me and - "

"Her courier? Mr Bulfinch, will you please explain

what you are talking about?" Braith turned square around and looked at him in a way that caused a still further diminution of his jauntiness and a proportionate increase of respect.

"Oh - I'll explain, if I know what you want explained. We were at Brindisi, were we not?"

"Yes."

"On our way to Cairo?"

"Yes."

"In the same hotel?"

"Yes."

"But I had no acquaintance with madame, and had only exchanged a word or two with you, when you were suddenly summoned to Paris by a telegram."

Braith bowed. He remembered well the false dispatch that had drawn him out of the way.

"Well, and when you left you told her you would be obliged to give up going to Cairo, and asked her to meet you in Vienna, whither you would have to go from Paris?"

"Oh, did I?"

"And you recommended a courier to her whom you knew very well, and in whom you had great confidence."

"Ah! And what was that courier's name?"

"Emanuel Pick. I wasn't fond of Emanuel myself," with a sharp glance at Braith's eyes, "but I supposed you knew something in his favor, or you would not have left - er - the lady in his charge."

Braith was silent.

"I understood him to be your agent," said the little man, cautiously.

"He was not."

"Oh!"

A long silence followed, during which Mr Bulfinch sought and found an explanation of several things. After a while he said musingly:

"I should like to meet Mr Pick again."

"Why should you want to meet him?"

"I wish to wring his nose two hundred times, one for each franc I lent him."

"How was that?" said Braith, absently.

"It was this way. He came to me and told me what I have repeated to you, and that you desired madame to go on at once and wait for you in Vienna, which you expected to reach in a few days after her arrival. That you had bought tickets - one first class for madame, two second class for him and for her maid - before you left, and had told her you had placed plenty of money for the other expenses in her dressing case. But this morning, on looking for the money, none could be found. Madame was sure it had not been stolen. She thought you must have meant to put it there, and forgotten afterwards. If she only had a few francs, just to last as far as Naples! Madame was well known to the bankers on the Santa Lucia there! etc. Well, I'm not such an ass that I didn't first see madame and get her to confirm his statement. But when she did confirm it, with such a charming laugh - she was very pretty - I thought she was a lady and your wife - "

In the midst of his bitterness, Braith could not help smiling at the thought of Nina with a maid and a courier. He remembered the tiny apartment in the Latin Quarter which she had been glad to occupy with him until conducted by her courier into finer ones. He made a gesture of disgust, and his face burned with the shame of a proud man who has received an affront from an inferior - and who knows it to be his own fault.

"I can at least have the satisfaction of setting that right," he said, holding two notes toward the little Mirror man, "and I can't thank you enough for giving me the opportunity."

Bulfinch drew back and stammered, "You don't think I spoke for that! You don't think I'd have spoken at all if I had known - "

"I do not. And I'm very glad you did not know, for it gives me a chance to clear myself. You must have thought me strangely forgetful, Mr Bulfinch, when the money was not repaid in due time."

"I - I didn't relish the manner in which you met me just now, I confess, but I'm very much ashamed of myself. I am indeed."

"Shake hands," said Braith, with one of his rare smiles.

The notes were left in Mr Bulfinch's fingers, and as he thrust them hastily out of sight, as if he truly was ashamed, he said, blinking up at Braith, "Do you - er - would you - may I offer you a glass of whiskey?" adding hastily, "I don't drink myself."

"Why, yes," said Braith, "I don't mind, but I won't drink all alone."

"Coffee is my tipple," said the other, in a faint voice.

"All right; suit yourself. But I should think that rather hot for such a day."

"Oh, I'll take it iced."

"Then let us walk over to the Café by the bandstand. We shall find the others somewhere about."

They strolled through the grove, past the music-stand, and sat down at one of the little iron tables under the trees. The band of the Garde Republicaine was playing. Bulfinch ordered sugar and Eau de selz for Braith, and iced coffee for himself.

Braith looked at the program: No. 1, Faust; No. 2, La Belle Hélène.

"Rex ought to be here, he's so fond of that."

Mr Bulfinch was mixing, in a surprisingly scientific manner for a man who didn't drink himself, something which the French call a "coquetelle"; a bit of ice, a little seltzer, a slice of lemon, and some Canadian Club whiskey. Braith eyed the well-worn flask.

"I see you don't trust to the Café's supplies."

"I only keep this for medicinal purposes," said the other, blinking nervously, "and - and I don't usually produce it when there are any newspapermen around."

"But you," said Braith, sipping the mixture with relish, "do you take none yourself?"

"I don't drink," said the other, and swallowed his coffee in such a hurry as to bring on a fit of coughing. Beads of perspiration clustered above his canary-colored eyebrows as he set down the glass with a gasp.

Braith was watching the crowd. Presently he exclaimed:

"There's Rex now," and rising, waved his glass and his cane and called Gethryn's name. The people sitting at adjacent tables glanced at one another resignedly. "More crazy English!"

"Rex! Clifford!" Braith shouted, until at last they heard him. In a few moments they had made their way through the crowd and sat down, mopping their faces and protesting plaintively against the heat.

Gethryn's glance questioned Braith, who said, "Mr Bulfinch and I have had the deuce of a time to make you fellows hear. You'd have been easier to call if you knew what sort of drink he can brew."

Clifford was already sniffing knowingly at the glass and turning looks of deep intelligence on Bulfinch, who responded gayly, "Hope you'll have some too," and with a sidelong blink at Gethryn, he produced the bottle, saying, "I don't drink myself, as Mr Gethryn knows."

Rex said, "Certainly not," not knowing what else to say. But the fondness of Clifford's gaze was ineffable.

Braith, who always hated to see Clifford look like that, turned to Gethryn. "Favorite of yours on the program."

Rex looked.

"Oh," he cried, "Belle Hélène." Next moment he flushed, and feeling as if the others saw it, crimsoned all the deeper. This escaped Clifford, however, who was otherwise occupied. But he joined in the conversation, hoping for an argument.

"Braith and Rex go in for the Meistersinger, Walküre, and all that rot - but I like some tune to my music."

"Well, you're going to get it now," said Braith; "the band are taking their places. Now for La Belle Hélène." He glanced at Gethryn, who had turned aside and leaned on the table, shading his eyes with his program.

The leader of the band stood wiping his mustache with one hand while he turned the leaves of his score with the other. The musicians came in laughing and chattering, munching their bit of biscuit or smacking their lips over lingering reminiscences of the intermission.

They hung their bayonets against the wall, and at the rat-tat of attention, came to order, standing in a circle with bugles and trombones poised and eyes fixed on the little gold-mounted baton.

A slow wave of the white-gloved hand, a few gentle tips of the wand, and then a sweep which seemed to draw out the long, rich opening chord of the Dream Song and set it drifting away among the trees till it lost itself in the rattle and clatter of the Boulevard St Michel.

Braith and Bulfinch set down their glasses and listened. Clifford silently blew long wreaths of smoke into the branches overhead. Gethryn leaned heavily on the table, one hand shading his eyes.

Oui c'est un rêve;
Un rêve doux d'amour -

The music died away in one last throb. Bulfinch sighed and blinked sentimentally, first on one, then on the other of his companions.

Suddenly the little Mirror man's eyes bulged out, he stiffened and grasped Braith's arm; his fingers were like iron.

"What the deuce!" began Braith, but, following the other's eyes, he became silent and stern.

"Talk of the devil - do you see him - Pick?"

"I see," growled Braith.

"And - and excuse me, but can that be madame? So like, and yet - "

Braith leaned forward and looked steadily at a couple who were slowly moving toward them in deep conversation.

"No," he said at last; and leaning back in his seat he refused to speak again.

Bulfinch chattered on excitedly, and at last he brought his fist down on the table at his right, where Clifford sat drawing a caricature on the marble top.

"I'd like," cried Bulfinch, "to take it out of his hide!"

"Hello!" said Clifford, disturbed in his peaceful occupation, "whose hide are you going to tan?"

"Nobody's," said Braith, sternly, still watching the couple who had now almost reached their group.

Clifford's start had roused Gethryn, who stirred and slowly looked up; at the same moment, the girl, now very near, raised her head and Rex gazed full into the eyes of Yvonne.

Her glance fell and the color flew to her temples. Gethryn's face lost all its color.

"Pretty girl," drawled Clifford, "but what a dirty little beggar she lugs about with her."

Pick heard and turned, his eyes falling first on Gethryn, who met his look with one that was worse than a kick. He glanced next at Braith, and then he turned green under the dirty yellow of the skin. Braith's eyes seemed to strike fire; his mouth was close set. The Jew's eyes shifted, only to fall on the pale, revengeful glare of T. Hoppley Bulfinch, who was half rising from his chair with all sorts of possibilities written on every feature.

"Let him go," whispered Braith, and turned his back.

Bulfinch sat down, his eyes like saucers. "I'd like - but not now!" he sputtered in a weird whisper.

Clifford had missed the whole thing. He had only eyes for the girl.

Gethryn sat staring after the couple, who were at that moment passing the gate into the Boulevard St Michel. He saw Yvonne stop and hastily thrust something into the Jew's hand, then, ignoring his obsequious salute, leave him and hurry down the Rue de Medicis.

The next Gethryn knew, Braith was standing beside him.

"Rex, will you join us at the Golden Pheasant for dinner?" was what he said, but his eyes added, "Don't let people see you look like that."

"I - I - don't know," said Gethryn. "Yes, I think so," with an effort.

"Come along, then!" said Braith to the others, and hurried them away.

Rex sat still till they were out of sight, then he got up and turned into the Avenue de l'Observatoire. He stopped and drank some cognac at a little café, and then started on, but he had no idea where he was going.

Presently he found himself crossing a bridge, and looked up. The great pile of Notre Dame de Paris loomed on his right. He crossed the Seine and wandered on without any aim - but passing the Tour St Jacques, and wishing to avoid the Boulevard, he made a sharp detour to the right, and after long wandering through byways and lanes, he crossed the foul, smoky Canal St Martin, and bore again to the right - always aimlessly.

Twilight was falling when his steps were arrested by fatigue. Looking up, he found himself opposite the gloomy mass of La Roquette prison. Sentinels slouched and dawdled up and down before the little painted sentry boxes under the great gate.

Over the archway was some lettering, and Gethryn stopped to read it:

La Roquette
Prison of the Condemned

He looked up and down the cheerless street. It was deserted save by the lounging sentinels and one wretched child, who crouched against the gateway.

"Fiche moi le camp! Allons! En route!" growled one of the sentinels, stamping his foot and shaking his fist at the bundle of rags.

Gethryn walked toward him.

"What's the matter with the little one?" he asked.

The soldier dropped the butt of his rifle with a ring, and said deferentially:

"Pardon, Monsieur, but the gamin has been here every day and all day for two weeks. It's disgusting."

"Is he hungry?"

"Ma foi? I can't tell you," laughed the sentry, shifting his weight to his right foot and leaning on the cross of his bayonet.

"Are you hungry, little one?" called Gethryn, pleasantly.

The child raised his head, with a wolfish stare, then sank it again and murmured: "I have seen him and touched him."

Gethryn turned to the soldier.

"What does he mean by that?" he demanded.

The sentry shrugged his shoulders. "He means he saw a hunchback. They say when one sees a hunchback and touches him, it brings good luck, if the hunchback is neither too old nor too young. Dame! I don't say there's nothing in it, but it can't save Henri Rigaud."

"And who is Henri Rigaud?"

"What! Monsieur has not heard of the affair Rigaud? Rigaud who did the double murder!"

"Oh, yes! In the Faubourg du Temple."

The sentry nodded. "He dies this week."

"And the child?"

"Is his."

Gethryn looked at the dirty little bundle of tatters.

"No one knows the exact day set for the affair, but," the sentry sank his voice to a whisper, "between you and me, I saw the widow going into the yard just before dinner, and Monsieur de Paris is here. That means tomorrow morning - click!"

"The - the widow?" repeated Gethryn.

"The guillotine. It will be over before this time tomorrow and the gamin there, who thinks the bossu will give him back his father - he'll find out his mistake, all in good time - all in good time!" and shouldering his rifle, the sentry laughed and resumed his slouching walk before the gateway.

Gethryn nodded to the soldier's salute and went up to the child, who stood leaning sullenly against the wall.

"Do you know what a franc is?" he asked.

The gamin eyed him doggedly.

"But I saw him," he said.

"Saw what?" said Gethryn, gently.

"The bossu," repeated the wretched infant vacantly.

"See here," said Gethryn, "listen to me. What would you do with twenty francs?"

"Eat, all day long, forever!"

Rex slipped two twenty-franc pieces into the filthy little fist.

"Eat," he murmured, and turned away.

Robert W. Chambers

Seven

Next morning, when Clifford arrived at the Atelier of MM. Boulanger and Lefebvre, he found the students more excited than usual over the advent of a "Nouveau."

Hazing at Julien's has assumed, of late, a comparatively mild form. Of course there are traditions of serious trouble in former years and a few fights have taken place, consequent upon the indignant resistance of new men to the ridiculous demands forced upon them by their ingenious tormentors. Still, the hazing of today is comparatively inoffensive, and there is not much of it. In the winter the students are too busy to notice a newcomer, except to make him feel strange and humble by their lofty scorn. But in the autumn, when the men have returned from their long out-of-door rest, with brush and palette, a certain amount of friskiness is developed, which sometimes expends itself upon the luckless "nouveau." A harmless search for the time-honored "grand reflecteur," an enforced song and dance, a stern command to tread the mazes of the shameless quadrille with an equally shameless model, is usually the extent of the infliction. Occasionally the stranger is invited to sit on a high stool and read aloud to the others while they work, as he would like to do himself. But sometimes, if a man resists these reasonable demands in a contumacious manner, he is "crucified." This occurs so seldom, however, that Clifford, on entering the barn-like studios that morning, was surprised to see that a "crucifixion" was in progress.

A stranger was securely strapped to the top rungs of a twenty-foot ladder which a crowd of Frenchmen were preparing to raise and place in a slanting position against the wall.

"Who is it that those fellows are fooling with?" he asked.

"An Englishman, and it's about time we put a stop to it," answered Elliott.

When Americans or Englishmen are hazed by the French students, they make common cause in keeping watch that the matter does not go too far.

"How many of us are here this morning?" said Clifford.

"Fourteen who can fight," said Elliott; "they only want someone to give the word."

Clifford buttoned his jacket and shouldered his way into the middle of the crowd. "That's enough. He's been put through enough for today," he said coolly.

A Frenchman, who had himself only entered the Atelier the week previous, laughed and replied, "We'll put you on, if you say anything."

There was an ominous pause. Every old student there

knew Clifford to be one of the most skillful and dangerous boxers in the school.

They looked with admiration upon their countryman. It didn't cost anything to admire him. They urged him on, and he didn't need much urging, for he remembered his own recent experience as a new man, and he didn't know Clifford.

"Go ahead," cried this misguided student, "he's a nouveau, and he's going up!"

Clifford laughed in his face. "Come along," he called, as some dozen English and American students pushed into the circle and gathered round the prostrate Englishman.

"See here, Clifford, what's the use of interrupting?" urged a big Frenchman.

Clifford began loosening the straps. "You know, Bonin, that we always do interfere when it goes as far as this against an Englishman or an American." He laughed good naturedly. "There's always been a fight over it before, but I hope there won't be any today."

Bonin grinned and shrugged his shoulders.

After vainly fussing with the ropes, Clifford and the others finally cut them and the "nouveau" scrambled to his feet and took an attitude which may be seen engraved in any volume of instruction in the noble art of self-defense. He was an Englishman of the sandy variety. Orange-colored whiskers decorated a carefully scrubbed face, terminating in a red-brown mustache. He had blue eyes, now lighted to a pale green by the fire of battle, reddish-brown hair, and white hands spattered with orange-colored freckles. All this, together with a well made suit of green and yellow checks, and the seesaw accent of the British Empire, answered, when politely addressed, to the name of Cholmondeley Rowden, Esq.

"I say," he began, "I'm awfully obliged, you know, and all that; but I'd jolly well like to give some of these cads a jolly good licking, you know."

"Go in, my friend, go in!" laughed Clifford; "but next time we'll leave you to hang in the air for an hour or two, that's all."

"Damn their cheek!" began the Englishman.

"See here," cried Elliott sharply, "you're only a nouveau, and you'd better shut up till you've been here long enough to talk."

"In other words," said Clifford, "don't buck against custom."

"But I cahn't see it," said the nouveau, brushing his dusty trousers. "I don't see it at all, you know. Damn their cheek!"

At this moment the week-weaned Frenchman shoved up to Clifford.

"What did you mean by interfering? Eh! You English pig."

Clifford looked at him with contempt. "What do you want, my little Nouveau?"

"Nouveau!" spluttered the Gaul, "Nouveau, eh!" and he made a terrific lunge at the American, who was sent stumbling backward, and slipping, fell heavily.

The Frenchman gazed around in triumph, but his grin was not reflected on the faces of his compatriots. None of them would have changed places with him.

Clifford picked himself up deliberately. His face was calm and mild as he walked up to his opponent, who hurriedly put himself into an attitude of self-defense.

"Monsieur Nouveau, you are not wise. But some day you will learn better, when you are no longer a nouveau," said Clifford, kindly. The man looked puzzled, but kept his fists up.

"Now I am going to punish you a little," proceeded Clifford, in even tones, "not harshly, but with firmness, for your good," he added, walking straight up to the Frenchman.

The latter struck heavily at Clifford's head, but he ducked like a flash, and catching his antagonist around the waist, carried him, kicking, to the water-basin, where he turned on the water and shoved the squirming Frenchman under. The scene was painful, but brief; when one of the actors in it emerged from under the water-spout, he no longer asked for anybody's blood.

"Go and dry yourself," said Clifford, cheerfully; and walking over to his easel, sat down and began to work.

In ten minutes, all trace of the row had disappeared, excepting that one gentleman's collar looked rather limp and his hair was uncommonly sleek. The men worked steadily. Snatches of song and bits of whistling rose continuously from easel and taboret, all blending in a drowsy hum. Gethryn and Elliott caught now and then, from behind them, words of wisdom which Clifford was administering to the now subdued Rowden.

"Yes," he was saying, "many a man has been injured for life by these Frenchmen for a mere nothing. I had two brothers," he paused, "and my golden-haired boy - " he ceased again, apparently choking with emotion.

"But - I say - you're not married, you know," said the Englishman.

"Hush," sighed Clifford, "I - I - married the daughter of an African duke. She was brought to the States by a slave trader in infancy."

"Black?" gasped Mr Rowden.

"Very black, but beautiful. I could not keep her. She left me, and is singing with Haverley's Minstrels now."

Like the majority of his countrymen, Mr Rowden was ready to believe anything he heard of social conditions in the States, but one point required explanation.

"You said the child had golden hair."

"Yes, his mother's hair was red," sighed Clifford.

Gethryn, glancing round, saw the Englishman's jaw drop, as he said, "How extraordinary!" Then he began to smile as if suspecting a joke. But Clifford's eye met his in gentle rebuke.

"C'est l'heure! Rest!" Down jumped the model. The men leaned back noisily. Clifford rose, bowed gravely to the Englishman, and stepped across the taborets to join his friends.

Gethryn was cleaning his brushes with turpentine and black soap.

"Going home, Rex?" inquired Clifford, picking up a brush and sending a fine spray of turpentine over Elliott, who promptly returned the attention.

"Quit that," growled Gethryn, "don't ruin those brushes."

"What's the nouveau like, Clifford?" asked Elliott. "We heard you instructing him a little. He seems to have the true Englishman's sense of humor."

"Oh, he's not a bad sort," said Clifford. "Come and be introduced. I'm half ashamed of myself for guying him, for he's really a very decent, plucky fellow, a bit stiff and pig-headed, as many of 'em are at first, and as for humor, I suppose they know their own kind, but they do get a little confused between fact and fancy when they converse with us."

The two strolled off with friendly intent, to seek out and ameliorate the loneliness of Cholmondeley Rowden, Esq.

Gethryn tied up his brushes, closed his color box and, flinging on his hat, hurried down the stairs and into the court, nodding to several students who passed with canvas and paint-boxes tucked under their arms. He reached the street, and, going through the Passage

Brady, emerged upon the Boulevard Sebastopol.

A car was passing and he boarded it, climbing up to the imperiale. The only vacant seat was between a great, red-faced butcher, and a market woman from the Halles, and although the odors of raw beef and fish were unpleasantly perceptible, he settled himself back and soon became lost in his own thoughts. The butcher had a copy of the Petit Journal and every now and then he imparted bits of it across Gethryn, to the market woman, lingering with relish over the criminal items.

"Dites donc," he cried, "here is the affair Rigaud!"

Gethryn roused up and listened.

"This morning, I knew it," cackled the woman, folding her fat hands across her apron. "I said to Sophie, `Voyons Sophie,' I said - "

"Shut up," interrupted the butcher, "I'm going to read."

"I was sure of it," said the woman, addressing Gethryn, "`Voyons, Sophie,' said - " but the butcher interrupted her, again reading aloud:

"The condemned struggled fearfully, and it required the united efforts of six gendarmes - "

"Cochon!" said the woman.

"Listen, will you!" cried the man. "Some disturbance was caused by a gamin who broke from the crowd and attacked a soldier. But the miserable was seized and carried off, screaming. Two gold pieces of 20 francs each fell from some hiding-place in his ragged clothes and were taken charge of by the police."

The man paused and gloated over the column. "Here," he cried, "Listen - `Even under the knife the condemned - '"

Gethryn rose roughly and, crowding past the man, descended the steps and, entering the car below, sat down there.

"Butor!" roared the butcher. "Cochon! He trod on my foot!"

"He is an English pig!" sneered the woman, reaching for the newspaper. "Let me read it now," she whined.

"Hands off," growled the man, "I'll read you what I think good."

"But it's my paper."

"It's mine now - shut up."

The first thing Gethryn did on reaching home was to write a note to his friend, the Prefect of the Seine, telling him how the child of Rigaud came by the gold pieces. Then he had a quiet smoke, and then he went out and lunched at the Café des Écoles, frugally, on a sandwich and a glass of beer. After that he returned to his studio and sat down to his desk again. He opened a small memorandum book and examined some columns of figures. They were rather straggling, not very well kept, but they served to convince him that his accounts were forty francs behind, and he would have to economize a little for the next week or two. After this, he sat and thought steadily. Finally he took a sheet of his best cream laid note paper, dipped his pen in the ink, and began to write. The note was short, but it took him a long while to compose it, and when it was sealed and directed to "Miss Ruth Deane, Lung' Arno Guicciardini, Florence, Italy," he sat holding it in his hand as if he did not know what to do with it.

Two o'clock struck. He started up, and quickly rolling up the shades from the glass roof and pulling out his easel, began to squeeze tube after tube of color upon his palette. The parrot came down and tiptoed about the floor, peering into color boxes, pastel cases, and pots of black soap, with all the curiosity of a regulation studio bore. Steps echoed on the tiles outside.

Gethryn opened the door quickly. "Ah, Elise! Bon jour!" he said, pleasantly. "Entrez donc!"

"Merci, Monsieur Gethryn," smiled his visitor, a tall, well-shaped girl with dark eyes and red cheeks.

"Ten minutes late," Elise, said Gethryn, laughing, "my time's worth a franc a minute; so prepare to pay up."

"Very well," retorted the girl, also laughing and showing her pretty teeth, "but I have decided to charge twenty francs an hour from today. Now, what do you owe me, Monsieur?"

Gethryn shook his brushes at her. "You are spoiled, Elise - you used to pose very well and were never late."

"And I pose well now!" she cried, her professional pride piqued. "Monsieur Bonnat and Monsieur Constant have praised me all this week. Voila," she finished, throwing off her waist and letting her skirts fall in a circle to her feet.

"Oh, you can pose if you will," answered Gethryn, pleasantly. "Come, we begin?"

The girl stepped daintily out of the pile of discarded clothes, and picking her way across the room with her bare feet, sprang lightly upon the model stand.

"The same as last week?" she asked, smiling frankly.

"Yes, that's it," he replied, shifting his easel and glancing up at the light; "only drop the left elbow a bit - there, that's it; now a little to the left - the knee - that will do."

The girl settled herself into the pose, glanced at the clock, and then turning to Gethryn said, "And I am to look at you, am I not?"

"Where could you find a more charming object?" murmured he, sorting his brushes.

"Thank you," she pouted, stealing a glance at him; "than you?"

"Except Mademoiselle Elise. There, now we begin!"

The rest of the hour was disturbed only by the sharp rattle of brushes and the scraping of the palette knife.

"Are you tired?" asked Gethryn, looking at the clock; "you have ten minutes more."

"No," said the girl, "continue."

Finally Gethryn rose and stepped back.

"Time," he said, still regarding his work. "Come and give me a criticism, Elise."

The girl stretched her limbs, and then, stepping down, trotted over to Gethryn.

"What do you say?" he demanded, anxiously.

Artists often pay more serious attention to the criticisms of their models than to those of a brother artist. For, although models may be ignorant of method - which, however, is not always the case - from seeing so much good work they acquire a critical acumen which often goes straight to the mark.

It was for one of these keen criticisms that the young man was listening now.

"I like it very much - very much," answered the girl, slowly; "but, you see - I am not so cold in the face - am I?"

"Hit it, as usual," muttered the artist, biting his lip; "I've got more greens and blues in there than there are in a peacock's tail. You're right," he added, aloud, "I must warm that up a bit - there in the shadows, and keep the high lights pure and cold."

Elise nodded seriously. "Monsieur Chaplain and I have finished our picture," she announced, after a pause.

It is a naïve way models have of appropriating work in which, truly enough, they have no small share. They often speak of "our pictures" and "our success."

"How do you like it?" asked the artist, absently.

"Good," - she shrugged her shoulders - "but not truth."

"Right again," murmured Gethryn.

"I prefer Dagnan," added the pretty critic.

"So do I - rather!" laughed Gethryn.

"Or you," said the girl.

"Come, come," cried the young man, coloring with pleasure, "you don't mean it, Elise!"

"I say what I mean - always," she replied, marching over to the pups and gathering them into her arms.

"I'm going to take a cigarette," she announced, presently.

"All right," said Gethryn, squeezing more paint on his palette, "you'll find some mild ones on the bookcase."

Elise gave the pups a little hug and kiss, and stepped lightly over to the bookcase. Then she lighted a cigarette and turned and surveyed herself in the mirror.

"I'm thinner than I was last year. What do you think?" she demanded, studying her pretty figure in the glass.

"Perhaps a bit, but it's all the better. Those corsets simply ruined you as a model last year."

Elise looked serious and shook her head.

"I do feel so much better without them. I won't wear them again."

"No, you have a pretty, slender figure, and you don't want them. That's why I always get you when I can. I hate to draw or paint from a girl whose hips are all discolored with ugly red creases from her confounded corset."

The girl glanced contentedly at her supple, clean-limbed figure, and then, with a laugh, jumped upon the model stand.

"It's not time," said Gethryn, "you have five minutes yet."

"Go on, all the same." And soon the rattle of the brushes alone broke the silence.

At last Gethryn rose and backed off with a sigh.

"How's that, Elise?" he called.

She sprang down and stood looking over his shoulder.

"Now I'm like myself!" she cried, frankly; "it's delicious! But hurry and block in the legs, why don't you?"

"Next pose," said the young man, squeezing out more color.

And so the afternoon wore away, and at six o'clock Gethryn threw down his brushes with a long-drawn breath.

"That's all for today. Now, Elise, when can you give me the next pose? I don't want a week at a time on this; I only want a day now and then."

The model went over to her dress and rummaged about in the pockets.

"Here," she said, handing him a notebook and diary.

He selected a date, and wrote his name and the hour.

"Good," said the girl, reading it; and replacing the book, picked up her stockings and slowly began to dress.

Gethryn lay back on the lounge, thoroughly tired out. Elise was humming a Normandy fishing song. When, at last, she stood up and drew on her gloves, he had fallen into a light sleep.

She stepped softly over to the lounge and listened to the quiet breathing of the young man.

"How handsome - and how good he is!" she murmured, wistfully.

She opened the door very gently.

"So different, so different from the rest!" she sighed, and noiselessly went her way.

Eight

Although the sound of the closing door was hardly perceptible, it was enough to wake Gethryn.

"Elise!" he called, starting up, "Elise!"

But the girl was beyond earshot.

"And she went away without her money, too; I'll drop around tomorrow and leave it; she may need it," he muttered, rubbing his eyes and staring at the door.

It was dinner time, and past, but he had little appetite.

"I'll just have something here," he said to himself, and catching up his hat ran down stairs. In twenty minutes he was back with eggs, butter, bread, a paté, a bottle of wine and a can of sardines. The spirit lamp was lighted and the table deftly spread.

"I'll have a cup of tea, too," he thought, shaking the blue tea canister, and then, touching a match to the well-filled grate, soon had the kettle fizzling and spluttering merrily.

The wind had blown up cold from the east and the young man shivered as he closed and fastened the

Robert W. Chambers

windows. Then he sat down, his chin on his hands, and gazed into the glowing grate. Mrs Gummidge, who had smelled the sardines, came rubbing up against his legs, uttering a soft mew from sheer force of habit. She was not hungry - in fact, Gethryn knew that the concierge, whose duty it was to feed all the creatures, overdid it from pure kindness of heart - at Gethryn's expense.

"Gummidge, you're stuffed up to your eyes, aren't you?" he said.

At the sound of his voice the cat hoisted her tail, and began to march in narrowing circles about her master's chair, making gentle observations in the cat language.

Gethryn placed a bit of sardine on a fork and held it out, but the little humbug merely sniffed at it daintily, and then rubbed against her master's hand.

He laughed and tossed the bit of fish into the fire, where it spluttered and blazed until the parrot woke up with a croak of annoyance. Gethryn watched the kettle in silence.

Faces he could never see among the coals, but many a time he had constructed animals and reptiles from the embers, and just now he fancied he could see a resemblance to a shark among the bits of blazing coal.

He watched the kettle dreamily. The fire glowed and flashed and sank, and glowed again. Now he could distinctly see a serpent twisting among the embers. The clock ticked in measured unison with the slow oscillation of the flame serpent. The wind blew hard against the panes and sent a sudden chill creeping to his feet.

Bang! Bang! went the blinds. The hallway was full of strange noises. He thought he heard a step on the threshold; he imagined that his door creaked, but he did not turn around from his study of the fire; it was the wind, of course.

The sudden hiss of the kettle, boiling over, made him jump and seize it. As he turned to set it down, there was a figure standing beside the table. Neither spoke. The kettle burnt his hand and he set it back on the hearth; then he remained standing, his eyes fixed on the fire.

After a while Yvonne broke the silence - speaking very low: "Are you angry?"

"Why?"

"I don't know," said the girl, with a sigh.

The silence was too strained to last, and finally Gethryn said, "Won't you sit down?"

She did so silently.

"You see I'm - I'm about to do a little cooking," he said, looking at the eggs.

The girl spoke again, still very low.

"Won't you tell me why you are angry?"

"I'm not," began Gethryn, but he sat down and glanced moodily at the girl.

"For two weeks you have not been to see me."

"You are mistaken, I have been - " he began, but stopped.

"When?"

"Saturday."

"And I was not at home?"

"And you were at home," he said grimly. "You had a caller - it was easy to hear his voice, so I did not knock."

She winced, but said quietly, "Don't you think that is rude?"

"Yes," said Gethryn, "I beg pardon."

Presently she continued: "You and - and he - are the only two men who have been in my room."

"I'm honored, I'm sure," he answered, drily.

The girl threw back her mackintosh and raised her veil.

"I ask your pardon again," he said; "allow me to relieve you of your waterproof."

She rose, suffering him to aid her with her cloak, and then sat down and looked into the fire in her turn.

"It has been so long - I - I - hoped you would come."

"Whom were you with in the Luxembourg Gardens?" he suddenly broke out.

She did not misunderstand or evade the question, and Gethryn, watching her face, thought perhaps she had expected it. But she resented his tone.

"I was with a friend," she said, simply.

He came and sat down opposite her.

"It is not my business," he said, sulkily; "excuse me."

She looked at him for some moments in silence.

"It was Mr Pick," she said at length.

Gethryn could not repress a gesture of disgust.

"And that - Jew was in your rooms? That Jew!"

"Yes." She sat nervously rolling and unrolling her gloves. "Why do you care?" she asked, looking into the fire.

"I don't."

"You do."

There was a pause.

"Rex," she said, very low, "will you listen?"

"Yes, I'll listen."

"He is a - a friend of my sister's. He came from her to - to - "

"To what!"

"To - borrow a little money. I distrusted him the first time he came - the time you heard him in my room - and I refused him. Saturday he stopped me in the street, and, hoping to avoid a chance of meeting - you, I walked through the park."

"And you gave him the money - I saw you!"

"I did - all I could spare."

"Is he - is your sister married?"

"No," she whispered.

"And why - " began Gethryn, angrily, "Why does that scoundrel come to beg money - " He stopped, for the girl was in evident distress.

"Ah! You know why," she said in a scarce audible voice.

The young man was silent.

"And you will come again?" she asked timidly.

No answer.

She moved toward the door.

"We were such very good friends."

Still he was silent.

"Is it au revoir?" she whispered, and waited for a moment on the threshold.

"Then it is adieu."

"Yes," he said, huskily, "that is better."

She trembled a little and leaned against the doorway.

"Adieu, mon ami - " She tried to speak, but her voice broke and ended in a sob.

Then, all at once, and neither knew just how it was, she was lying in his arms, sobbing passionately.

*

"Rex," said Yvonne, half an hour later, as she stood before the mirror arranging her disordered curls, "are you not the least little bit ashamed of yourself?"

The answer appeared to be satisfactory, but the curly head was in a more hopeless state of disorder than before, and at last the girl gave a little sigh and exclaimed, "There! I'm all rumpled, but its your fault. Will you oblige me by regarding my hair?"

"Better let it alone; I'll only rumple it some more!" he cried, ominously.

"You mustn't! I forbid you!"

"But I want to!"

"Not now, then - "

"Yes - immediately!"

"Rex - you mustn't. O, Rex - I - I - "

"What?" he laughed, holding her by her slender wrists.

She flushed scarlet and struggled to break away.

"Only one."

"No."

"One."

"None."

"Shall I let you go?"

"Yes," she said, but catching sight of his face, stopped short.

He dropped her hands with a laugh and looked at her. Then she came slowly up to him, and flushing crimson, pulled his head down to hers.

"Yvonne, do you love me? Truthfully?"

"Rex, can you ask?" Her warm little head lay against his throat, her heart beat against his, her breath fell upon his cheek, and her curls clustered among his own.

"Yvonne - Yvonne," he murmured, "I love you - once and forever."

"Once and forever," she repeated, in a half whisper.

"Forever," he said.

*

An hour later they were seated tete-à-tete at Gethryn's little table. She had not permitted him to poach the eggs, and perhaps they were better on that account.

"Bachelor habits must cease," she cried, with a little laugh, and Gethryn smiled in doubtful acquiescence.

"Do you like grilled sardines on toast?" she asked.

"I seem to," he smiled, finishing his fourth; "they are delicious - yours," he added.

"Oh, that tea!" she cried, "and not one bit of sugar. What a hopelessly careless man!"

But Gethryn jumped up, crying, "Wait a moment!" and returned triumphantly with a huge mass of rock-candy - the remains of one of Clifford's abortive attempts at "rye-and-rock."

They each broke off enough for their cups, and Gethryn, tasting his, declared the tea "delicious." Yvonne sat, chipping an egg and casting sidelong glances at Gethryn, which were always met and returned with interest.

"Yvonne, I want to tell you a secret."

"What, Rex?"

"I love you."

"Oh!"

"And you?"

"No - not at all!" cried the girl, shaking her pretty head. Presently she gave him a swift glance from beneath her drooping lashes.

"Rex?"

"What, Yvonne?"

"I want to tell you a secret."

"What, Yvonne?"

"If you eat so many sardines - "

"Oh!" cried Gethryn, half angrily, but laughing, "you must pay for that!"

"What?" she said, innocently, but jumped up and kept the table between him and herself.

"You know!" he cried, chasing her into a corner.

"We are two babies," she said, very red, following him back to the table. The paté was eaten in comparative quiet.

"Now," she said, with great dignity, setting down her glass, "behave and get me some hot water."

Gethryn meekly brought it.

"If you touch me while I am washing these dishes!"

"But let me help?"

"No, go and sit down instantly."

He fled in affected terror and ensconced himself upon the sofa. Presently he inquired, in a plaintive voice: "Have you nearly finished?"

"No," said the girl, carefully drying and arranging the quaint Egyptian tea-set, "and I won't for ages."

"But you're not going to wash all those things? The concierge does that."

"No, only the wine-glasses and the tea-set. The idea of trusting such fragile cups to a concierge! What a boy!"

But she was soon ready to dry her slender hands, and caught up a towel with a demure glance at Gethryn.

"Which do you think most of - your dogs, or me?"

"Pups."

"That parrot, or me?"

"Poll."

"The raven, or me? The cat, or me?"

"Bird and puss."

She stole over to his side and knelt down.

"Rex, if you ever tire of me - if you ever are unkind - if you ever leave me - I think I shall die."

He drew her to him. "Yvonne," he whispered, "we can't always be together."

"I know it - I'm foolish," she faltered.

"I shall not always be a student. I shall not always be in Paris, dear Yvonne."

She leaned closer to him.

"I must go back to America someday."

"And - and marry?" she whispered, chokingly.

"No - not to marry," he said, "but it is my home."

"I - I know it, Rex, but don't let us think of it. Rex," she said, some moments after, "are you like all students?"

"How do you mean?"

"Have you ever loved - before - a girl, here in Paris - like me?"

"There are none - like you."

"Answer me, Rex."

"No, I never have," he said, truthfully. Presently he added, "And you, Yvonne?"

She put her warm little hand across his mouth.

"Don't ask," she murmured.

"But I do!" he cried, struggling to see her eyes, "won't you tell me?"

She hid her face tight against his breast.

"You know I have; that is why I am alone here, in Paris."

"You loved him?"

"Yes - not as I love you."

Presently she raised her eyes to his.

"Shall I tell you all? I am like so many - so many others. When you know their story, you know mine."

He leaned down and kissed her.

"Don't tell me," he said.

But she went on.

"I was only seventeen - I am nineteen now. He was an officer at - at Chartres, where we lived. He took me to Paris."

"And left you."

"He died of the fever in Tonquin."

"When?"

"Three weeks ago."

"And you heard?"

"Tonight."

"Then he did leave you."

"Don't, Rex - he never loved me, and I - I never really loved him. I found that out."

"When did you find it out?"

"One day - you know when - in a - a cab."

"Dear Yvonne," he whispered, "can't you go back to - to your family?"

"No, Rex."

"Never?"

"I don't wish to, now. No, don't ask me why! I can't tell you. I am like all the rest - all the rest. The Paris fever is only cured by death. Don't ask me, Rex; I am content - indeed I am."

Suddenly a heavy rapping at the door caused Gethryn to spring hurriedly to his feet.

"Rex!"

It was Braith's voice.

"What!" cried Gethryn, hoarsely.

There was a pause.

"Aren't you going to let me in?"

"I can't, old man; I - I'm not just up for company tonight," stammered Gethryn.

"Company be damned - are you ill?"

"No."

There was a silence.

"I'm sorry," began Gethryn, but was cut short by a gruff:

"All right; good night!" and Braith went away.

Yvonne looked inquiringly at him.

"It was nothing," he murmured, very pale, and then threw himself at her feet, crying, "Oh, Yvonne - Yvonne!"

Outside the storm raged furiously.

Presently she whispered, "Rex, shall I light the candle? It is midnight."

"Yes," he said.

She slipped away, and after searching for some time, cried, "the matches are all gone, but here is a piece of paper - a letter; do you want it? I can light it over the lamp."

She held up an envelope to him.

"I can light it over the lamp," she repeated.

"What is the address?"

"It is very long; I can't read it all, only

`Florence, Italy.'"

"Burn it," he said, in a voice so low she could scarcely hear him.

Presently she came over and knelt down by his side. Neither spoke or moved.

"The candle is lighted," she whispered, at last.

"And the lamp?"

"Is out."

Nine

Cholmondeley Rowden had invited a select circle of friends to join him in a "petit diner a la stag," as he expressed it.

Eight months of Paris and the cold, cold world had worked a wonderful change in Mr Rowden. For one thing, he had shaved his whiskers and now wore only a mustache. For another, he had learned to like and respect a fair portion of the French students, and in consequence was respected and liked in return.

He had had two fights, in both of which he had contributed to the glory of the British Empire and prize ring.

He was a better sparrer than Clifford and was his equal in the use of the foils. Like Clifford, he was a capital banjoist, but he insisted that cricket was far superior to baseball, and this was the only bone of contention that ever fell between the two.

Clifford played his shameless jokes as usual, accompanied by the enthusiastic applause of Rowden. Clifford also played "The Widow Nolan's Goat" upon his banjo, accompanied by the intricate pizzicatos of Rowden.

Robert W. Chambers

Clifford drank numerous bottles of double X with Rowden, and Rowden consumed uncounted egg-flips with Clifford. They were inseparable; in fact, the triumvirate, Clifford, Elliott and Rowden, even went so far as to dress alike, and mean-natured people hinted that they had but one common style in painting. But they did not make the remark to any of the triumvirate. They were very fond of each other, these precious triumvirs, but they did not address each other by nicknames, and perhaps it was because they respected each other enough to refrain from familiarities that this alliance lasted as long as they lived.

It was a beautiful sight, that of the three youths, when they sallied forth in company, hatted, clothed, and gloved alike, and each followed by a murderous-looking bulldog. The animals were of the brindled variety, and each was garnished with a steel spiked collar. Timid people often crossed to the other side of the street on meeting this procession.

Braith laughed at the whole performance, but secretly thought that a little of their spare energy and imagination might have been spent to advantage upon their artistic productions.

Braith was doing splendidly. His last year's picture had been hung on the line and, in spite of his number three, he had received a third class medal and had been praised - even generously - by artists and critics, including Albert Wolff. He was hard at work on a large canvas for the coming International Exhibition at Paris; he had sold a number of smaller studies, and besides had pictures well hung in Munich and in more than one gallery at home.

At last, after ten years of hard work, struggles, and disappointments, he began to enjoy a measure of success. He and Gethryn saw little of each other this winter, excepting at Julien's. That last visit to the Rue Monsieur le Prince was never mentioned between them. They were as cordial when they met as ever, but Braith did not visit his young friend any more, and Gethryn never spoke to him of Yvonne.

"Good-bye, old chap!" Braith would say when they parted, gripping Rex's hand and smiling at him. But Rex did not see Braith's face as he walked away.

Braith felt helpless. The thing he most dreaded for Rex had happened; he believed he could see the end of it all, and yet he could prevent nothing. If he should tell Rex that he was being ruined, Rex would not listen, and - who was he that he should preach to another man for the same fault by which he had wasted his own life? No, Rex would never listen to him, and he dreaded a rupture of their friendship.

Gethryn had made his debut in the Salon with a certain amount of éclat. True, he had been disappointed in his expectations of a medal, but a first mention had soothed him a little, and, what was more important, it proved to be the needed sop to his discontented aunt. But somehow or other his new picture did not progress rapidly, or in a thoroughly satisfactory manner. In bits and spots it showed a certain amount of feverish brilliancy, yes, even mature solidity; in fact, it was nowhere bad, but still it was not Gethryn and he knew that.

"Confound it!" he would mutter, standing back from his canvas; but even at such times he could hardly help wondering at his own marvelous technique.

"Technique be damned! Give me stupidity in a pupil every time, rather than cleverness," Harrington had said to one of his pupils, and the remark often rang in Gethryn's ears even when his eyes were most blinded by his own wonderful facility.

"Some fools would medal this," he thought; "but what pleasure could a medal bring me when I know how little I deserve it?"

Perhaps he was his own hardest critic, but it was certain that the old, simple honesty, the subtle purity, the almost pathetic effort to tell the truth with paint and brush, had nearly disappeared from Gethryn's canvases during the last eight months, and had given place to a fierce and almost startling brilliancy, never, perhaps, hitting, but always threatening some brutal note of discord.

Even Elise looked vaguely troubled, though she always smiled brightly at Gethryn's criticism of his own work.

"It is so very wonderful and dazzling, but - but the color seems to me - unkind."

And he would groan and answer, "Yes, yes, Elise, you're right; oh, I can never paint another like the one of last June!"

"Ah, that!" she would cry, "that was delicious - " but checking herself, she would add, "Courage, let us try again; I am not tired, indeed I am not."

Yvonne never came into the studio when Gethryn had

models, but often, after the light was dim and the models had taken their leave, she would slip in, and, hanging lightly over his shoulder, her cheek against his, would stand watching the touches and retouches with which the young artist always eked out the last rays of daylight. And when his hand drooped and she could hardly distinguish his face in the gathering gloom, he would sigh and turn to her, smoothing the soft hair from her forehead, saying: "Are you happy, Yvonne?" And Yvonne always answered, "Yes, Rex, when you are."

Then he would laugh, and kiss her and tell her he was always happy with La Belle Hélène, and they would stand in the gathering twilight until a gurgle from the now well-grown pups would warn them that the hour of hunger had arrived.

The triumvirate, with Thaxton, Rhodes, Carleton, and the rest, had been frequent visitors all winter at the "Ménagerie," as Clifford's bad pun had named Gethryn's apartment; but, of late, other social engagements and, possibly, a small amount of work, had kept them away. Clifford was a great favorite with Yvonne. Thaxton and Elliott she liked. Rowden she tormented, and Carleton she endured. She captured Clifford by suffering him to play his banjo to her piano. Rowden liked her because she was pretty and witty, though he never got used to her quiet little digs at his own respected and dignified person. Clifford openly avowed his attachment and spent many golden hours away from work, listening to her singing. She had been taught by a good master and her voice was pure and pliant, although as yet only half developed. The little concerts they gave their friends were really charming - with Clifford's banjo, Gethryn's guitar, Thaxton's violin, Yvonne's voice and piano. Clifford made the programs. They were profusely illustrated, and he spent a great deal of time rehearsing, writing verses, and rehashing familiar airs (he called it "composing") which would have been as well devoted to his easel.

In Rowden, Yvonne was delighted to find a cultivated musician. Clifford listened to their talk of chords and keys, went and bought a "Musical Primer" on the Quai d'Orsay, spent a wretched hour groping over it, swore softly, and closed the book forever.

But neither the triumvirate nor the others had been to the "Ménagerie" for over a fortnight, when Rowden, feeling it incumbent upon him to return some of Gethryn's hospitality, issued very proper cards - indeed they were very swell cards for the Latin Quarter - for a "dinner," to be followed by a "quiet evening" at the Bal Masqué at the Opera.

The triumvirate had accordingly tied up their brindled bulldogs, "Spit," "Snap" and "Tug"; had donned their white ties and collars of awful altitude, and were fully prepared to please and to be pleased. Although it was nominally a "stag" party, the triumvirate would as soon have cut off their tender mustaches as have failed to invite Yvonne. But she had replied to Rowden's invitation by a dainty little note, ending:

> and I am sure that you will understand when I say that this time I will leave you gentlemen in undisturbed possession of the evening, for I know how dearly men love to meet and behave like bears all by themselves. But I shall see you all afterward at the Opera. Au revoir then - at the Bal Masqué. Y.D.

The first sensation to the young men was one of disappointment. But the second was that Mademoiselle Descartes' tact had not failed her.

The triumvirate were seated upon the sideboard swinging their legs. Rowden cast a satisfied glance at the table laid for fifteen and flicked an imaginary speck from his immaculate shirt front.

"I think it's all right," said Elliott, noticing his look, "eh, Clifford?"

"Is there enough champagne?" asked that youth, calculating four quart bottles to each person.

Rowden groaned.

"Of course there is. What are you made of?"

"Human flesh," acknowledged the other meekly.

At eleven the guests began to arrive, welcomed by the triumvirs with great state and dignity. Rowden, looking about, missed only one - Gethryn, and he entered at the same moment.

"Just in time," said Rowden, and made the move to the table. As Gethryn sat down, he noticed that the place on Rowden's right was vacant, and before it stood a huge bouquet of white violets.

"Too bad she isn't here," said Rowden, glancing at Gethryn and then at the vacant place.

"That's awfully nice of you, Rowden," cried Gethryn, with a happy smile; "she will have a chance to thank you tonight."

He leaned over and touched his face to the flowers. As he raised his head again, his eyes met Braith's.

"Hello!" cried Braith, cordially.

Rex did not notice how pale he was, and called back, "Hello!" with a feeling of relief at Braith's tone. It was always so. When they were apart for days, there weighed a cloud of constraint on Rex's mind, which Braith's first greeting always dispelled. But it gathered again in the next interval. It rose from a sullen deposit of self-reproach down deep in Gethryn's own heart. He kept it covered over; but he could not prevent the ghost-like exhalations that gathered there and showed where it was hidden.

Speeches began rather late. Elliott made one - and offered a toast to "la plus jolie demoiselle de Paris," which was drunk amid great enthusiasm and responded to by Gethryn, ending with a toast to Rowden. Rowden's response was stiff, but most correct. The same could not be said of Clifford's answer to the toast, "The struggling Artist - Heaven help him!"

Towards 1 am Mr Clifford's conversation had become incoherent. But he continued to drink toasts. He drank Yvonne's health five times, he pledged Rowden and Gethryn and everybody else he could think of, down to Mrs Gummidge and each separate kitten, and finally pledged himself. By that time he had reached the lachrymose state. Tears, it seemed, did him good. A heart-rending sob was usually the sign of reviving intelligence.

"Well," said Gethryn, buttoning his greatcoat, "I'll see you all in an hour - at the Opera."

Braith was not coming with them to the Ball, so Rex shook hands and said "Good night," and calling "Au revoir" to Rowden and the rest, ran down stairs three at a time. He hurried into the court and after spending five minutes shouting "Cordon!" succeeded in getting out of the door and into the Rue Michelet. From there he turned into the Avenue de l'Observatoire, and cutting through into the Boulevard, came to his hôtel.

Yvonne was standing before the mirror, tying the hood of a white silk domino under her chin. Hearing Gethryn's key in the door, she hurriedly slipped on her little white mask and confronted him.

"Why, who is this?" cried Gethryn. "Yvonne, come and tell me who this charming stranger is!"

"You see before you the Princess Hélène, Monsieur, she said, gravely bending the little masked head."

"Oh, in that case, you needn't come, Yvonne, as I have an engagement with the Princess Hélène of Troy."

"But you mustn't kiss me!" she cried, hastily placing the table between herself and Gethryn; "you have not yet been presented. Oh, Rex! Don't be so - so idiotic; you spoil my dress - there - yes, only one, but don't you dare to try - Oh Rex! Now I am all in wrinkles - you - you bear!"

"Bears hug - that's a fact," he laughed. "Come, are you ready - or I'll just - "

"Don't you dare!" she cried, whipping off her mask and attempting an indignant frown. She saw the big bunch of white violets in his hand and made a diversion by asking what those were. He told her, and she declared, delightedly, that she should carry them with Rex's roses to the Ball.

"They shall have the preference, Monsieur," she said, teasingly. "Oh, Rex! don't - please - " she entreated.

"All right, I won't," he said, drawing her wrap around her; and Yvonne, replacing the mask and gathering up her fluffy skirts, slipped one small gloved hand through his arm and danced down the stairs.

On the corner of the Vaugirard and the Rue de Medicis one always finds a line of cabs, and presently they were bumping and bouncing away down the Rue de Seine to the river.

Je fais ce que sa fantaisie
  Veut m'ordonner,
Et je puis, s'il lui faut ma vie
  La lui donner

sang Yvonne, deftly thrusting tierce and quarte with her fan to make Gethryn keep his distance.

"Do you know it is snowing?" he said presently, peering out of the window as the cab rattled across the Pont Neuf.

"Tant mieux!" cried the girl; "I shall make a snowball - a - " she opened her blue eyes impressively, "a very, very large one, and - "

"And?"

"Drop it on the head of Mr Rowden," she announced, with cheerful decision.

"I'll warn poor Rowden of your intention," he laughed, as the cab rolled smoothly up the Avenue de l'Opera, across the Boulevard des Italiens, and stopped before the glittering pile of the great Opera.

She sprang lightly to the curbstone and stood tapping her little feet against the pavement while Gethryn fumbled about for his fare.

The steps of the Opera and the Plaza were covered with figures in dominoes, blue, red or black, many grotesque and bizarre costumes, and not a few sober claw hammers. The great flare of yellow light which bathed and flooded the shifting, many-colored throng, also lent a strangely weird effect to the now heavily falling snowflakes. Carriages and cabs kept arriving in countless numbers. It was half past two, and nobody who wanted to be considered anybody thought of arriving before that hour. The people poured in a steady stream through the portals. Groups of English and American students in their irreproachable evening attire, groups of French students in someone else's doubtful evening attire, crowds of rustling silken dominoes, herds of crackling muslin dominoes, countless sad-faced Pierrots, fewer sad-faced Capuchins, now and then a slim Mephistopheles, now and then a fat, stolid Turk, 'Arry, Tom, and Billy, redolent of plum pudding and Seven Dials, Gontran, Gaston and Achille, savoring of brasseries and the Sorbonne. And then, from the carriages and fiacres: Mademoiselle Patchouli and good old Monsieur

Robert W. Chambers

Bonvin, Mademoiselle Nitouche and bad young Monsieur de Sacrebleu, Mademoiselle Moineau and Don Cæsar Imberbe; and the pink silk domino of "La Pataude" - mais n'importe!

Allons, Messieurs, Mesdames, to the cloak room - to the foyer! To the escalier! or you, Madame la Comtesse, to your box, and smooth out your crumpled domino; as for "La Pataude," she is going to dance tonight.

Gethryn, with Yvonne clinging tightly to his arm, entered the great vestibule and passed through the railed lanes to the broad inclined aisle which led to the floor.

"Do you want to take a peep before we go to our box?" he asked, leading her to the doorway.

Yvonne's little heart beat faster as she leaned over and glanced at the dazzling spectacle.

"Come, hurry - let us go to the box!" she whispered, dragging Gethryn after her up the stairway.

He followed, laughing at her excitement, and in a few minutes they found the door of their lodge and slipped in.

Gethryn lighted a cigarette and began to unstrap his field glasses.

"Take these, Yvonne," he said, handing them to her while he adjusted her own tiny gold ones.

Yvonne's cheeks flushed and her eyes sparkled under

the little mask, as she leaned over the velvet railing and gazed at the bewildering spectacle below. Great puffs of hot, perfumed air bore the crash of two orchestras to their ears, mixed with the distant clatter and whirl of the dancers, and the shouts and cries of the maskers.

At the end of the floor, screened by banks of palms, sat the musicians, and round about, rising tier upon tier, the glittering boxes were filled with the elite of the demimonde, who ogled and gossiped and sighed, entirely content with the material and social barriers which separate those who dance for ten francs from those who look on for a hundred.

But there were others there who should not by any means be confounded with their sisters of the "half-world."

The Faubourg St Germain, the Champs Elysées, and the Parc Monceau were possibly represented among those muffled and disguised beauties, who began the evening with their fans so handy in case of need. Ah, well - now they lay their fans down quite out of reach in case of emergency, and who shall say if disappointment lurks under these dainty dominoes, that there is so little to bring a blush to modest cheeks - alas! few emergencies.

And you over there - you of the "American Colony," who are tossed like shuttlecocks in the social whirl, you, in your well-appointed masks and silks, it is all very new and exciting - yes, but why should you come? American women, brought up to think clean thoughts and see with innocent eyes, to exact a respectful homage from men and enjoy a personal dignity and independence unknown to women anywhere else - why do you want to come here? Do you not know that the foundations of that liberty which makes you envied in the old world are laid in the respect and confidence of men? Undermine that, become wise and cynical, learn the meaning of doubtful words and gestures whose significance you never need have suspected, meet men on the same ground where they may any day meet fast women of the continent, and fix at that moment on your free limbs the same chains which corrupt society has forged for the women of Europe.

Yvonne leaned back in her box with a little gasp.

"But I can't make out anyone at all," she said; "it's all a great, sparkling sea of color."

"Try the field glasses," replied Gethryn, giving them to her again, at the same time opening her big plumy fan and waving it to and fro beside the flushed cheek.

Presently she cried out, "Oh, look! There is Mr Elliott and Mr Rowden, and I think Mr Clifford - but I hope not."

He leaned forward and swept the floor with the field glass.

"It's Clifford, sure enough," he muttered; "what on earth induces him to dance in that set?"

It was Clifford.

At that moment he was addressing Elliott in pleading, though hazy, phrases.

"Come 'long, Elliott, don't be so - so uncomf't'ble 'n' p'tic'lar! W't's use of be'ng shnobbish?" he urged, clinging hilariously to his partner, a pigeon-toed ballet girl. But Elliott only laughed and said:

"No; waltzes are all I care for. No quadrille for me - "

The crash of the orchestra drowned his voice, and Clifford, turning and bowing gravely to his partner, and then to his vis-à-vis, began to perform such antics and cut such pigeonwings that his pigeon-toed partner glared at him through the slits of her mask in envious astonishment. The door was dotted with numerous circles of maskers, ten or fifteen deep, all watching and applauding the capers of the hilarious couples in the middle.

But Clifford's set soon attracted a large and enthusiastic audience, who were connoisseurs enough to distinguish a voluntary dancer from a hired one; and when the last thundering chords of Offenbach's "March into Hell" scattered the throng into a delirious waltz, Clifford reeled heavily into the side scenes and sat down, rather unexpectedly, in the lap of Mademoiselle Nitouche, who had crept in there with the Baron Silberstein for a nice, quiet view of a genuine cancan.

Mademoiselle did not think it funny, but the Baron did, and when she boxed Clifford's ears he thought it funnier still.

Rowden and Elliot, who were laboriously waltzing with a twin pair of flat-footed Watteau Shepherdesses, immediately ran to his assistance; and later, with a plentiful application of cold water and still colder air, restored Mr Clifford to his usual spirits.

"You're not a beauty, you know," said Rowden, looking at Clifford's hair, which was soaked into little points and curls; "you're certainly no beauty, but I think you're all right now - don't you, Elliott? "

"Certainly," laughed the triumvir, producing a little silver pocket-comb and presenting it to the woebegone Clifford, who immediately brought out a hand glass and proceeded to construct a "bang" of wonderful seductiveness.

In ten minutes they sallied forth from the dressing room and wended their way through the throngs of masks to the center of the floor. They passed Thaxton and Rhodes, who, each with a pretty nun upon his arm, were trying to persuade Bulfinch into taking the third nun, who might have been the Mother Superior or possibly a resuscitated 14th century abbess.

"No," he was saying, while he blinked painfully at the ci-devant abbess, "I can't go that; upon my word, don't ask me, fellows - I - I can't."

"Oh, come," urged Rhodes, "what's the odds?"

"You can take her and I'll take yours," began the wily little man, but neither Rhodes nor Thaxton waited to argue longer.

"No catacombs for me," growled Bulfinch, eyeing the retreating nuns, but catching sight of the triumvirate, his face regained its bird-like felicity of expression.

"Glad to see you - indeed I am! That Colossus is too disinterested in securing partners for his friends; he is, I assure you. If you're looking for a Louis Quatorze partner, warranted genuine, go to Rhodes."

"Rex ought to be here by this time," said Rowden; "look in the boxes on that side and Clifford and I will do the same on this."

"No need," cried Elliott, "I see him with a white domino there in the second tier. Look! he's waving his hand to us and so is the domino."

"Come along," said Clifford, pushing his way toward the foyer, "I'll find them in a moment. Let me see," - a few minutes later, pausing outside a row of white and gilt doors - "let me see, seventh box, second tier - here we are," he added, rapping loudly.

Yvonne ran and opened the door.

"Bon soir, Messieurs," she said, with a demure curtsy.

Clifford gallantly kissed the little glove and then shook hands with Gethryn.

"How is it on the floor?" asked the latter, as Elliott and Rowden came forward to the edge of the box. "I want to take Yvonne out for a turn and perhaps a waltz, if it isn't too crowded."

"Oh, it's pretty rough just now, but it will be better in half an hour," replied Rowden, barricading the champagne from Clifford.

"We saw you dancing, Mr Clifford," observed Yvonne, with a wicked glance at him from under her mask.

Clifford blushed.

"I - I don't make an ass of myself but once a year, you know," he said, with a deprecatory look at Elliott.

"Oh," murmured the latter, doubtfully, "glad to hear it."

Clifford gazed at him in meek reproof and then made a flank movement upon the champagne, but was again neatly foiled by Rowden.

Yvonne looked serious, but presently leaned over and filled one of the long-stemmed goblets.

"Only one, Mr Clifford; one for you to drink my health, but you must promise me truthfully not to take any more wine this evening!"

Clifford promised with great promptness, and taking the glass from her hand with a low bow, sprang recklessly upon the edge of the box and raised the goblet.

"A la plus belle demoiselle de Paris!" he cried, with all the strength of his lungs, and drained the goblet.

A shout from the crowd below answered his toast. A thousand faces were turned upward, and people leaned over their boxes, and looked at the party from all parts of the house.

Mademoiselle Nitouche turned to Monsieur de Sacrebleu.

"What audacity!" she murmured.

Mademoiselle Goujon smiled at the Baron Silberstein.

"Tiens!" she cried, "the gayety has begun, I hope."

Little Miss Ducely whispered to Lieutenant Faucon:

"Those are American students," she sighed; "how jolly they seem to be, especially Mr Clifford! I wonder if she is so pretty!"

Half a dozen riotous Frenchmen in the box opposite jumped to their feet and waved their goblets at Clifford.

"A la plus jolie femme du monde!" they roared.

Clifford seized another glass and filled it.

"She is here!" he shouted, and sprang to the edge again. But Gethryn pulled him down.

"That's too dangerous," he laughed; "you could easily fall."

"Oh, pshaw!" cried Clifford, draining the glass, and shaking it at the opposite box.

Yvonne put her hand on Gethryn's arm.

"Don't let him have any more," she whispered.

"Give us the goblet!" yelled the Frenchmen.

"Le voila!" shouted Clifford, and stepping back, hurled the glass with all his strength across the glittering gulf. It fell with a crash in the box it was aimed at, and a howl of applause went up from the floor.

Yvonne laughed nervously, but coming to the edge of the box buried her mask in her bouquet and looked down.

"A rose! A rose!" cried the maskers below; "a rose from the most charming demoiselle in Paris!"

She half turned to Gethryn, but suddenly stepping forward, seized a handful of flowers from the middle of the bouquet and flung them into the crowd.

There was a shout and a scramble, and then she tore the bouquet end from end, sending a shower of white buds into the throng.

"None for me?" sighed Clifford, watching the fast-dwindling bouquet.

She laughed brightly as she tossed the last handful below, and then turned and leaned over Gethryn's chair.

"You destructive little wretch!" he laughed, "this is not the season for the Battle of Flowers. But white roses mean nothing, so I'm not jealous."

"Ah, mon ami, I saved the red rose for you," she whispered; and fastened it upon his breast.

And at his whispered answer her cheeks flushed crimson under the white mask. But she sprang up laughing.

"I would so like to go onto the floor," she cried, pulling him to his feet, and coaxing him with a simply irresistible look; "don't you think we might - just for a minute, Mr Rowden?" she pleaded. "I don't mind a crowd - indeed I don't, and I am masked so perfectly."

"What's the harm, Rex?" said Rowden; "she is well masked."

"And when we return it will be time for supper, won't it?"

"Yes, I should think so!" murmured Clifford.

"Where do we go then?"

"Maison Dorée."

"Come along, then, Mademoiselle Destructiveness!" cried Gethryn, tossing his mask and field glass onto a chair, where they were appropriated by Clifford, who spent the next half hour in staring across at good old Colonel Toddlum and his frisky companion - an attention which drove the poor old gentleman almost frantic with suspicion, for he was a married man, bless his soul! - and a pew-holder in the American Church.

"My love," said the frisky one, "who is the gentleman in the black mask who stares?"

"I don't know," muttered the dear old man, in a cold sweat, "I don't know, but I wish I did."

And the frisky one shrugged her shoulders and smiled at the mask.

"What are they looking at?" whispered Yvonne, as she tripped along, holding very tightly to Gethryn's arm.

"Only a quadrille - `La Pataude' is dancing. Do you want to see it?"

She nodded, and they approached the circle in the middle of which `La Pataude' and `Grille d'Egout' were holding high carnival. At every
ostentatious display of hosiery the crowd roared.

"Brava! Bis!" cried an absinthe-soaked old gentleman; "vive La Pataude!"

For answer the lady dexterously raised his hat from his head with the point of her satin slipper.

The crowd roared again. "Brava! Brava, La Pataude!"

Yvonne turned away.

"I don't like it. I don't find it amusing," she said, faintly.

Gethryn's hand closed on hers.

"Nor I," he said.

"But you and your friends used to go to the students' ball at `Bullier's,'" she began, a little reproachfully.

"Only as Nouveaux, and then, as a rule, the high-jinks are pretty genuine there - at least, with the students. We used to go to keep cool in spring and hear the music; to keep warm in winter; and amuse ourselves at Carnival time."

"But - Mr Clifford knows all the girls at `Bullier's.' Do - do you?"

"Some."

"How many?" she said, pettishly.

"None - now."

A pause. Yvonne was looking down.

"See here, little goose, I never cared about any of that crowd, and I haven't been to the Bullier since - since last May."

She turned her face up to his; tears were stealing down from under her mask.

"Why, Yvonne!" he began, but she clung to his shoulder, as the orchestra broke into a waltz.

"Don't speak to me, Rex - but dance! Dance!"

They danced until the last bar of music ceased with a thundering crash.

"Tired?" he asked, still holding her.

She smiled breathlessly and stepped back, but stopped short, with a little cry.

"Oh! I'm caught - there, on your coat!"

He leaned over her to detach the shred of silk.

"Where is it? Oh! Here!"

And they both laughed and looked at each other, for she had been held by the little golden clasp, the fleur-de-lis.

"You see," he said, "it will always draw me to you."

But a shadow fell on her fair face, and she sighed as she gently took his arm.

When they entered their box, Clifford was still tormenting the poor Colonel.

"Old dog thinks I know him," he grinned, as Yvonne and Rex came in. Yvonne flung off her mask and began to fan herself.

"Time for supper, you know," suggested Clifford.

Yvonne lay back in her chair, smiling and slowly waving the great plumes to and fro.

"Who are those people in the next box?" she asked him. "They do make such a noise."

"There are only two, both masked."

"But they have unmasked now. There are their velvets on the edge of the box. I'm going to take a peep," she whispered, rising and leaning across the railing.

"Don't; I wouldn't - " began Gethryn, but he was too late.

Yvonne leaned across the gilded cornice and instantly fell back in her chair, deathly pale.

"My God! Are you ill, Yvonne?"

"Oh, Rex, Rex, take me away - home - "

Then came a loud hammering on the box door. A harsh, strident voice called, "Yvonne! Yvonne!"

Clifford thoughtlessly threw it open, and a woman in evening dress, very decolletée, swept by him into the box, with a waft of sickly scented air.

Yvonne leaned heavily on Gethryn's shoulder; the woman stopped in front of them.

"Ah! here you are, then!"

Yvonne's face was ghastly.

"Nina," she whispered, "why did you come?"

"Because I wanted to make you a little surprise," sneered the woman; "a pleasant little surprise. We love each other enough, I hope." She stamped her foot.

"Go," said Yvonne, looking half dead.

"Go!" mimicked the other. "But certainly! Only first you must introduce me to these gentlemen who are so kind to you."

"You will leave the box," said Gethryn, in a low voice, holding open the door.

The woman turned on him. She was evidently in a prostitute's tantrum of malicious deviltry. Presently she would begin to lash herself into a wild rage.

"Ah! this is the one!" she sneered, and raising her

voice, she called, "Mannie, Mannie, come in here, quick!"

A sidling step approached from the next box, and the face of Mr Emanuel Pick appeared at the door.

"This is the one," cried the woman, shrilly. "Isn't he pretty?"

Mr Pick looked insolently at Gethryn and opened his mouth, but he did not say anything, for Rex took him by the throat and kicked him headlong into his own box. Then he locked the door, and taking out the key, returned and presented it to the woman.

"Follow him!" he said, and quietly, but forcibly, urged her toward the lobby.

"Mannie! Mannie!" she shrieked, in a voice choked by rage and dissipation, "come and kill him! He's insulting me!"

Getting no response, she began to pour forth shriek upon shriek, mingled with oaths and ravings. "I shall speak to my sister! Who dares prevent me from speaking to my sister! You - " she glared at Yvonne and ground her teeth. "You, the good one. You! the mother's pet! Ran away from home! Took up with an English hog!"

Yvonne sprang to her feet again.

"Leave the box," she gasped.

"Ha! ha! Mais oui! leave the box! and let her dance while her mother lies dying!"

Yvonne gave a cry.

"Ah! Ah!" said her sister, suddenly speaking very slowly, nodding at every word. "Ah! Ah! go back to your room and see what is there - in the room of your lover - the little letter from Vernon. She wants you. She wants you. That is because you are so good. She does not want me. No, it is you who must come to see her die. I - I dance at the Carnival!"

Then, suddenly turning on Gethryn with a devilish grin, "You! tell your mistress her mother is dying!" She laughed hatefully, but preserved her pretense of calm, walked to the door, and as she reached it swung round and made an insulting gesture to Gethryn.

"You! I will remember you!"

The door slammed and a key rattled in the next box.

Clinging to Gethryn, Yvonne passed down the long corridor to the vestibule, while Elliott and Rowden silently gathered up the masks and opera glasses. Clifford stood holding her crushed and splintered fan. He looked at Elliott, who looked gloomily back at him, as Braith entered hurriedly.

"What's the matter? I saw something was wrong from the floor. Rex ill?"

"Ill at ease," said Clifford, grimly. "There's a sister turned up. A devil of a sister."

Braith spoke very low. "Yvonne's sister?"

"Yes, a she-devil."

"Did you hear her name?"

"Name's Nina."

Braith went quietly out again. Passing blindly down the lobby, he ran against Mr Bulfinch. Mr Bulfinch was in charge of a policeman.

"Hello, Braith!" he called, hilariously.

Braith was going on with a curt nod when the other man added:

"I've taken it out of Pick," and he stopped short. "I got my two hundred francs worth," the artist of the London Mirror proceeded, "and now I shall feel bound to return you yours - the first time I have it," he ended, vaguely.

Braith made an impatient gesture.

"Are you under arrest?"

"Yes, I am. He couldn't help it," smiling agreeably at the Sergeant de Ville. "He saw me hit him."

The policeman looked stolid.

"But what excuse?" began Braith.

"Oh! none! Pick just passed me, and I felt as if I couldn't stand it any longer, so I pitched in."

"Well, and now you're in for fine and imprisonment."

"I suppose so," said Bulfinch, beaming.

"Have you any money with you?"

"No, unless I have some in your pocket?" said the little man, with a mixture of embarrassment and bravado that touched Braith, who saw what the confession cost him.

"Lots!" said he, cordially. "But first let us try what we can do with Bobby. Do you ever drink a petit verre, Monsieur le Sergeant de Ville?" with a winning smile to the wooden policeman.

The latter looked at the floor.

"No," said he.

"Never?"

"Never!"

"Well, I was only thinking that over on the Corner of the Rue Taitbout one finds excellent wine at twenty francs."

The officer now gazed dreamily at the ceiling.

"Mine costs forty," he said.

And a few minutes later the faithful fellow stood in front of the Opera house quite alone.

Ten

The cab rolled slowly over the Pont au Change, and the wretched horse fell into a walk as he painfully toiled up the hill of St Michel. Yvonne lay back in the corner; covered with all her own wraps and Gethryn's overcoat, she shivered.

"Poor little Yvonne!" was all he said as he leaned over now and then to draw the cloak more closely around her. Not a sound but the rumble of the wheels and the wheezing of the old horse broke the silence. The streets were white and deserted. A few ragged flakes fell from the black vault above, or were shaken down from the crusted branches.

The cab stopped with a jolt. Yvonne was trembling as Rex lifted her to the ground, and he hurried her into the house, up the black stairway and into their cold room.

When he had a fire blazing in the grate, he looked around. She was kneeling on the floor beside a candle she had lighted, and her tears were pouring down upon the page of an open letter. Rex stepped over and touched her.

"Come to the fire." He raised her gently, but she could not stand, and he carried her in his arms to the great soft chair before the grate. Then he knelt down and warmed her icy hands in his own. After a while he moved her chair back, and drawing off her dainty white slippers, wrapped her feet in the fur that lay heaped on the hearth. Then he unfastened the cloak and the domino, and rolling her gloves from elbow to wrist, slipped them over the helpless little hands. The firelight glanced and glowed on her throat and bosom, tingeing their marble with opalescent lights, and searching the deep shadows under her long lashes. It reached her hair, touching here and there a soft, dark wave, and falling aslant the knots of ribbon on her bare shoulders, tipped them with points of white fire.

"Is it so bad, dearest Yvonne?"

"Yes."

"Then you must go?"

"Oh, yes!"

"When?"

"At daylight."

Gethryn rose and went toward the door; he hesitated, came back and kissed her once on the forehead. When the door closed on him she wept as if her heart would break, hiding her head in her arms. He found her lying so when he returned, and, throwing down her traveling bag and rugs, he knelt and took her to his breast, kissing her again and again on the forehead. At last he had to speak.

"I have packed the things you will need most and will

send the rest. It is getting light, dearest; you have to change your dress, you know."

She roused herself and sat up, looking desolately about her.

"Forever!" she whispered.

"No! No!" cried Gethryn.

"Ah! oui, mon ami!"

Gethryn went and stood by the window. The bedroom door was closed.

Day was breaking. He opened the window and looked into the white street. Lamps burned down there with a sickly yellow; a faint light showed behind the barred windows of the old gray barracks. One or two stiff sparrows hopped silently about the gutters, flying up hurriedly when the frost-covered sentinel stamped his boots before the barracks gate. Now and then a half-starved workman limped past, his sabots echoing on the frozen pavement. A hooded and caped policeman, a red-faced cabman stamping beside his sleepy horse - the street was empty but for them.

It grew lighter. The top of St Sulpice burned crimson. Far off a bugle fluttered, and then came the tramp of the morning guard mount. They came stumbling across the stony court and leaned on their rifles while one of them presented arms and received the word from the sentry. Little by little people began to creep up and down the sidewalks, and the noise of wooden shutters announced another day of toil begun. The point of the Luxembourg Palace struck fire as the ghastly gas-lamps faded and went out. Suddenly the great bell of St Sulpice clashed the hour - Eight o'clock!

Again a bugle blew sharply from the barracks, and a troop of cavalry danced and pawed through the gate, clattering away down the Rue de Seine.

Gethryn shut the window and turned into the room. Yvonne stood before the dying embers. He went to her, almost timidly. Neither spoke. At last she took up her satchel and wrap.

"It is time," she whispered. "Let us go."

He clasped her once in his arms; she laid her cheek against his.

*

The train left Montparnasse station at nine. There was hardly anyone in the waiting room. The Guard flung back the grating.

"Vernon, par Chartres?" asked Gethryn.

"Vernon - Moulins - Chartres - direct!" shouted the Guard, and stamped off down the platform.

Gethryn showed his ticket which admitted him to the platform, and they walked slowly down the line of dismal-looking cars.

"This one?" and he opened a door.

She stood watching the hissing and panting engine, while Gethryn climbed in and placed her bags and rugs in a window corner. The car smelt damp and musty, and he stepped out with a choking sensation in his chest. A train man came along, closing doors with a slam.

"All aboard - ladies - gentlemen - voyageurs?" he growled, as if to himself or some familiar spirit, and jerked a sullen clang from the station bell. The engine panted impatiently.

Rex struggled against the constraint that seemed to be dividing them.

"Yvonne, you will write?"

"I don't know!"

"You don't know! Yvonne!"

"I know nothing except that I am wicked, and my mother is dying!" She said it in low, even tones, looking away from him.

The gong struck again, with a startling clash.

The engine shrieked; a cloud of steam rose from under the wheels. Rex hurried her into the carriage; there was no one else there. Suddenly she threw herself into his arms.

"Oh! I love you! I love you! One kiss, no; no; on the lips. Good-bye, my own Rex!"

"You will come again?" he said, crushing her to him.

Her eyes looked into his.

"I will come. I love you! Be true to me, Rex. I will come back."

Her lover could not speak. Doors slamming, and an impatient voice - "Descendez donc, M'sieu!" - roused him; he sprang from the carriage, and the train rolled slowly out of the smoke-filled station.

How heavy the smoke was! Gethryn could hardly breathe - hardly see. He walked away and out into the street. The city was only half awake even yet. After, as it seemed, a long time, he found himself looking at a clock which said a quarter past ten. The winter sunshine slanted now on roof and pane, flooding the western side of the shabby boulevard, dappling the snow with yellow patches. He had stopped in the chilly shadow of a gateway and was looking vacantly about. He saw the sunshine across the street and shivered where he was, and yet he did not leave the shadow. He stood and watched the sparrows taking bold little baths in the puddles of melted snow water. They seemed to enjoy the sunshine, but it was cold in the shade, cold and damp - and the air was hard to breathe. A policeman sauntered by and eyed him curiously. Rex's face was haggard and pinched. Why had he stood there in the cold for half an hour, without ever changing his weight from one foot to the other?

The policeman spoke at last, civilly:

"Monsieur!"

Gethryn turned his head.

"Is it that Monsieur seeks the train?" he asked, saluting.

Rex looked up. He had wandered back to the station. He lifted his hat and answered with the politeness dear to French officials.

"Merci, Monsieur!" It made him cough to speak, and he moved on slowly.

Gethryn would not go home yet. He wanted to be where there was plenty of cool air, and yet he shivered. He drew a deep breath which ended in a pain. How cold the air must be - to pain the chest like that! And yet, there were women wheeling handcarts full of yellow crocus buds about. He stopped and bought some for Yvonne.

"She will like them," he thought. "Ah!" - he turned away, leaving flowers and money. The old flower-woman crossed herself.

No - he would not go home just yet. The sun shone brightly; men passed, carrying their overcoats on their arms; a steam was rising from the pavements in the Square.

There was a crowd on the Pont au Change. He did not see any face distinctly, but there seemed to be a great many people, leaning over the parapets, looking down the river. He stopped and looked over too. The sun glared on the foul water eddying in and out among the piles and barges. Some men were rowing in a boat, furiously. Another boat followed close. A voice close by Gethryn cried, angrily:

"Dieu! who are you shoving?"

Rex moved aside; as he did so a gamin crowded

quickly forward and craned over the edge, shouting, "Vive le cadavre!"

"Chut!" said another voice.

"Vive la Mort! Vive la Morgue!" screamed the wretched little creature.

A policeman boxed his ears and pulled him back. The crowd laughed. The voice that had cried, "Chut!" said lower, "What a little devil, that Rigaud!"

Rex moved slowly on.

In the Court of the Louvre were people enough and to spare. Some of them bowed to him; several called him to turn and join them. He lifted his hat to them all, as if he knew them, but passed on without recognizing a soul. The broad pavements were warm and wet, but the air must have been sharp to hurt his chest so. The great pigeons of the Louvre brushed by him. It seemed as if he felt the beat of their wings on his brains. A shabby-looking fellow asked him for a sou - and, taking the coin Rex gave him, shuffled off in a hurry; a dog followed him, he stooped and patted it; a horse fell, he went into the street and helped to raise it. He said to a man standing by that the harness was too heavy - and the man, looking after him as he walked away, told a friend that there was another crazy foreigner.

Soon after this he found himself on the Quai again, and the sun was sinking behind the dome of the Invalides. He decided to go home. He wanted to get warm, and yet it seemed as if the air of a room would stifle him. However, once more he crossed the Seine, and as he turned in at his own gate he met Clifford, who said something, but Rex pushed past without trying to understand what it was.

He climbed the dreary old stairs and came to his silent studio. He sat down by the fireless hearth and gazed at a long, slender glove among the ashes. At his feet her little white satin slippers lay half hidden in the long white fur of the rug.

He felt giddy and weak, and that hard pain in his chest left him no peace. He rose and went into the bedroom. Her ball dress lay where she had thrown it. He flung himself on the bed and buried his face in the rustling silk. A faint odor of violets pervaded it. He thought of the bouquet that had been placed for her at the dinner. Then the flowers reminded him of last summer. He lived over again their gay life - their excursions to Meudon, Sceaux, Versailles with its warm meadows, and cool, dark forests; Fontainebleau, where they lunched under the trees; St Cloud - Oh! he remembered their little quarrel there, and how they made it up on the boat at Suresnes afterward.

He rose excitedly and went back into the studio; his cheeks were aflame and his breath came sharp and hard. In a corner, with its face to the wall, stood an old, unfinished portrait of Yvonne, begun after one of those idyllic summer days.

When Braith walked in, after three times knocking, he found Gethryn painting feverishly by the last glimmer of daylight on this portrait. The room was full of shadows, and while they spoke it grew quite dark.

That night Braith sat by his side and listened to his incoherent talk, and Dr White came and said

"Pleuro-pneumonia" was what ailed him. Braith had his traps fetched from his own place and settled down to nurse him.

Eleven

C arnival was over. February had passed, like January, for most of the fellows, in a bad dream of unpaid bills. March was going in much the same way. This is the best account Clifford, Elliott and Rowden could have given of it. Thaxton and Rhodes were working. Carleton was engaged to a new pretty girl - the sixth or seventh.

Satan found the time passing delightfully. There was no one at present to restrain him when he worried Mrs Gummidge. The tabby daily grew thinner and sadder-eyed. The parrot grew daily more blasé. He sneered more and more bitterly, and his eyelid, when closed, struck a chill to the soul of the raven.

At first the pups were unhappy. They missed their master. But they were young, and flies were getting plentiful in the studio.

For Braith the nights and the days seemed to wind themselves in an endless chain about Rex's sickbed. But when March had come and gone Rex was out of danger, and Braith began to paint again on his belated picture. It was too late, now, for the Salon; but he wanted to finish it all the same.

One day, early in April, he came back to Gethryn after an unusually long absence at his own studio.

Rex was up and trying to dress. He turned a peaked face toward his friend. His eyes were two great hollows, and when he smiled and spoke, in answer to Braith's angry exclamation, his jaws worked visibly.

"Keep cool, old chap!" he said, in the ghost of a voice.

"What are you getting up for, all alone?"

"Had to - tired of the bed. Try it yourself - six weeks!"

"You want to go back there and never quit it alive - that's what you want," said Braith, nervously.

"Don't, either. Come and button this collar and stop swearing."

"I suppose you're going back to Julien's the day after tomorrow," said Braith, sarcastically, after Rex was dressed and had been helped to the lounge in the studio.

"No," said he, "I'm going to Arcachon tomorrow."

"Arca - - twenty thousand thunders!"

"Not at all," smiled Rex - a feeble, willful smile.

Braith sat down and drew his chair beside Gethryn.

"Wait a while, Rex."

"I can't get well here, you know."

"But you can get a bit stronger before you start on such a journey."

"I thought the doctor told you the sooner I went south the better."

That was true; Braith was silent a while.

At last he said, "I have all the money you will want till your own comes, you know, and I can get you ready by the end of this week, if you will go."

Rex was no baby, but his voice shook when he answered.

"Dear old, kind, unselfish friend! I'd almost rather remain poor, and let you keep on taking care of me, but - see here - " and he handed him a letter. "That came this morning, after you left."

Braith read it eagerly, and looked up with a brighter face than he had worn for many a day.

"By Jove!" he said. "By Jupiter!"

Rex smiled sadly at his enthusiasm.

"This means health, and a future, and - everything to you, Rex!"

"Health and wealth, and happiness," said Gethryn bitterly.

"Yes, you ungrateful young reprobate - that's exactly what it means. Go to your Arcachon, by all means, since you've got a fortune to go on - I say - you - you didn't know your aunt very well, did you? You're not cut up much?"

"I never saw her half a dozen times in my whole life. But she's been generous to me, poor old lady!"

"I should think so. Two hundred and fifty thousand dollars is a nice sum for a young fellow to find in his pocket all on a sudden. And now - you want to go away and get well, and come back presently and begin where you left off - a year ago. Is that it?"

"That is it. I shall never get well here, and I mean to get well if I can," - he paused, and hesitated. "That was the only letter in my box this morning."

Braith did not answer.

"It is nearly two months now," continued Rex, in a low voice.

"What are your plans?" interrupted Braith, brusquely.

Rex flushed.

"I'm going first" - he answered rather drily, "to Arcachon. You see by the letter my aunt died in Florence. Of course I've got to go and measure out a lot of Italian red tape before I can get the money. It seems to me the sooner I can get into the pine air and the sea breezes at Arcachon, the better chance I have of being fit to push on to Florence, via the Riviera, before the summer heat."

"And then?"

"I don't know."

"You will come back?"

"When I am cured."

There was a long silence. At last Gethryn put a thin hand on Braith's shoulder and looked him lovingly in the face.

"You know, and I know, how little I have ever done to deserve your goodness, to show my gratitude and - and love for you. But if I ever come back I will prove to you - "

Braith could not answer, and did not try to. He sat and looked at the floor, the sad lines about his mouth deeply marked, his throat moving once or twice as he swallowed the lump of grief that kept rising.

After a while he muttered something about its being time for Rex's supper and got up and fussed about with a spirit lamp and broths and jellies, more like Rex's mother than a rough young bachelor. In the midst of his work there came a shower of blows on the studio door and Clifford, Rowden and Elliott trooped in without more ado.

They set up a chorus of delighted yells at seeing Rex dressed and on the studio lounge. But Braith suppressed them promptly.

"Don't you know any better than that?" he growled. "What did you come for, anyway? It's Rex's supper time."

"We came, Papa," said Clifford, "to tell Rex that I have reformed. We wanted him to know it as soon as we did ourselves."

"Ah! he's a changed man! He's worked all day at Julien's for a week past," cried Elliott and Rowden together.

"And my evenings?" prompted Clifford sweetly.

"Are devoted to writing letters home!" chanted the chorus.

"Get out!" was all Rex answered, but his face brightened at the three bad boys standing in a row with their hats all held politely against their stomachs. He had not meant to tell them, dreading the fatigue of explanations, but by an impulse he held out his hand to them.

"I say, you fellows, shake hands! I'm going off tomorrow."

Their surprise having been more or less noisily and profusely expressed, Braith stepped decidedly in between them and his patient, satisfied their curiosity, and gently signified that it was time to go.

He only permitted one shake apiece, foiling all Clifford's rebellious attempts to dodge around him and embrace Gethryn. But Rex was lying back by this time, tired out, and he was glad when Braith closed the studio door. It flew open the next minute and an envelope came spinning across to Rex.

"Letter in your box, Reggy - good-bye, old chap!" said

Clifford's voice.

The door did not quite close again and the voices and steps of his departing friends came echoing back as Braith raised a black-edged letter from the floor. It bore the postmark: Vernon.

Twelve

R ound about the narrow valley which is cut by the rapid Trauerbach, Bavarian mountains tower, their well timbered flanks scattered here and there with rough slides, or opening out in long green alms, and here at evening one may sometimes see a spot of yellow moving along the bed of a half dry mountain torrent.

Miss Ruth Dene stood in front of the Forester's lodge at Trauerbach one evening at sunset, and watched such a spot on the almost perpendicular slope that rose opposite, high above her head. Some Jaegers and the Forester were looking, too.

"My glass, Federl! Ja! 's ist'n gams!"

"Gems?" inquired Miss Dene, excited by her first view of a chamois.

"Ja! 'n Gams," said the Forester, sticking to his dialect.

The sun was setting behind the Red Peak, his last rays pouring into the valley. They fell on rock and alm, on pine and beech, and turned the silver Trauerbach to molten gold.

Mr Isidor Blumenthal, sitting at a table under one of the windows, drinking beer, beheld this phenomenon, and putting down his quart measure, he glared at the waste of precious metal. Then he lighted the stump of a cigar; then he looked at his watch, and it being almost supper time, he went in to secure the best place. He liked being early at table; he liked the first cut of the meats, hot and fat; he loved plenty of gravy. While waiting to be served he could count the antlers on the walls and estimate "how much they would fetch by an antiquar," as he said to himself. There was nothing else marketable in the large bare room, full of deal tables and furnished with benches built against the wall. But he could pick his teeth demonstratively - toothpicks were not charged in the bill - and he could lean back on two legs of his chair, with his hands in his pockets, and stare through the windows at Miss Dene.

The Herr Förster and the two Jaegers had gone away. Miss Dene stood now with her slender hands clasped easily behind her, a Tam O'Shanter shading her sweet face. She was tall, and so far as Mr Blumenthal had ever seen, extremely grave for her years. But Mr Blumenthal's opportunities of observing Miss Dene had been limited.

The "gams" had disappeared. Miss Dene was looking down the road that leads to Schicksalsee. There was not much visible there except a whirl of dust raised by the sudden evening wind.

Sometimes it was swept away for a moment; then she saw a weather-beaten bridge and a bend in the road where it disappeared among the noble firs of a Bavarian forest.

The sun sank and left the Trauerbach a stream of molten lead. The shadows crept up to the Jaeger's hut and then to the little chapel above that. Gusts of whistling martins swept by.

A silk-lined, Paris-made wool dress rustled close beside her, and she put out one of the slender hands without turning her head.

"Mother, dear," said she, as a little silver-haired old lady took it and came and leaned against her tall girl's shoulder, "haven't we had enough of the `Först-haus zu Trauerbach?'"

"Not until a certain girl, who danced away her color at Cannes, begins to bloom again."

Ruth shrugged, and then laughed. "At least it isn't so – so indigestible as Munich."

"Oh! Absurd! Speaking of digestion, come to your Schmarn und Reh-braten. Supper is ready."

Mother and daughter walked into the dingy "Stube" and took their seats at the Forester's table.

Mr Blumenthal's efforts had not secured him a place there after all; Anna, the capable niece of the Frau Förster, having set down a large foot, clad in a thick white stocking and a carpet slipper, to the effect that there was only room for the Herr Förster's family and the Americans.

"I also am an American!" cried Mr Blumenthal in Hebrew-German. Nevertheless, when Ruth and her mother came in he bowed affably to them from the nearest end of the next table.

"Mamma," said Ruth, very low, "I hope I'm not going to begin being difficult, but do you know, that is really an odious man?"

"Yes, I do know," laughed her easy-tempered mother, "but what is that to us?"

Mr Blumenthal was reveling in hot fat. After he had bowed and smiled greasily, he tucked his napkin tighter under his chin and fell once more upon the gravy. He sopped his bread in it and scooped it up with his knife. But after there was no more gravy he wished to converse. He scrubbed his lips with one end of the napkin and called across to Ruth, who shrank behind her mother: "Vell, Miss Dene, you have today a shammy seen, not?"

Ruth kept out of sight, but Mrs Dene nodded, good-naturedly.

"Ja! soh! and haf you auch dose leetle deer mit der mamma seen? I haf myself such leetle deer myself many times shoot, me and my neffe. But not here. It is not permitted." No one answered. Ruth asked Anna for the salt.

"My neffe, he eats such lots of salt - " began Mr Blumenthal.

"Herr Förster," interrupted Mrs Dene - "Is the room ready for our friend who is coming this evening?"

"Your vriendt, he is from New York?"

"Ja, ja, Gnädige Frau!" said the Forester, hastily.

"I haf a broader in New York. Blumenthal and Cohen, you know dem, yes?"

Mrs Dene and her daughter rose and went quietly out into the porch, while the Frau Förster, with cold, round gray eyes and a tight mouth, was whispering to her frowning spouse that it was none of his business, and why get himself into trouble? Besides, Mrs Dene's Herr Gemahl, meaning the absent colonel, would come back in a day or two; let him attend to Mr Blumenthal.

Outside, under the windows, were long benches set against the house with tables before them. One was crowded with students who had come from everywhere on the foot-tours dear to Germans.

Their long sticks, great bundles, tin botanizing boxes, and sketching tools lay in untidy heaps; their stone krugs were foaming with beer, and their mouths were full of black bread and cheese.

Underneath the other window was the Jaeger's table. There they sat, gossiping as usual with the Forester's helpers, a herdsman or two, some woodcutters on their way into or out from the forest, and a pair of smart revenue officers from the Tyrol border, close by.

Ruth said to the nearest Jaeger in passing:

"Herr Loisl, will you play for us?"

"But certainly, gracious Fraulein! Shall I bring my zither to the table under the beech tree?"

"Please do!"

Miss Dene was a great favorite with the big blond Jaegers.

"Ja freili! will I play for the gracious Fraulein!" said Loisl, and cut slices with his hunting knife from a large white radish and ate them with black bread, shining good-humor from the tip of the black-cock feather on his old green felt hat to his bare, bronzed knees and his hobnailed shoes.

At the table under the beech trees were two more great fellows in gray and green. They rose promptly and were moving away; Mrs Dene begged them to remain, and they sat down again, diffidently, but with dignity.

"Herr Sepp," said Ruth, smiling a little mischievously, "how is this? Herr Federl shot a stag of eight this morning, and I hear that yesterday you missed a Reh-bock!"

Sepp reddened, and laughed. "Only wait, gracious Fraulein, next week it is my turn on the Red Peak."

"Ach, ja! Sepp knows the springs where the deer drink," said Federl.

"And you never took us there!" cried Ruth, reproach-fully. "I would give anything to see the deer come and drink at sundown."

Sepp felt his good breeding under challenge. "If the gracious Frau permits," with a gentlemanly bow to Mrs Dene, "and the ladies care to come - but the way is hard - "

"You couldn't go, dearest," murmured Ruth to her mother, "but when papa comes back - "

"Your father will be delighted to take you wherever there is a probability of breaking both your necks, my dear," said Mrs Dene.

"Griffin!" said Ruth, giving her hand a loving little squeeze under the table.

Loisl came up with his zither and they all made way before him. Anna placed a small lantern on the table and the light fell on the handsome bearded Jaeger's face as he leaned lovingly above his instrument.

The incurable "Sehnsucht" of humanity found not its only expression in that great Symphony where "all the mightier strings assembling, fell a trembling." Ruth heard it as she leaned back in the deep shade and listened to those silvery melodies and chords of wonderful purity, coaxed from the little zither by Loisl's strong, rough hand, with its tender touch. To all the airs he played her memory supplied the words. Sometimes a Sennerin was watching from the Alm for her lover's visit in the evening. Sometimes the hunter said farewell as he sprang down the mountainside. Once tears came into Ruth's eyes as the simple tune recalled how a maiden who died and went to Heaven told her lover at parting:

"When you come after me I shall know you by my ring which you will wear, and me you will know by your rose that rests on my heart."

Loisl had stopped playing and was tuning a little, idly sounding chords of penetrating sweetness. There came a noise of jolting and jingling from the road below.

Mrs Dene spoke softly to Ruth. "That is the Mail; it is time he was here." Ruth assented absently. She cared at that moment more for hearing a new folk-song than for the coming of her old playmate.

Rapid wheels approaching from the same direction overtook and passed the "Post" and stopped below. Mrs Dene rose, drawing Ruth with her. The three tall Jaegers rose too, touching their hats. Thanking them all, with a special compliment to Loisl, the ladies went and stood by some stone steps which lead from the road to the Först-haus, just as a young fellow, proceeding up them two at a time, arrived at the top, and taking Mrs Dene's hand began to kiss it affectionately.

"At last!" she cried, "and the very same boy! after four years! Ruth!" Ruth gave one hand and Reginald Gethryn took two, releasing one the next moment to put his arm around the little old lady, and so he led them both into the house, more at home already than they were.

"Shall we begin to talk about how we are not one bit changed, only a little older, first, or about your supper?" said Mrs Dene.

"Oh! supper, please!" said Rex, of the sun-browned face and laughing eyes. Smiling Anna, standing by, understood, aided by a hint from Ruth of "Schmarn und Reh-braten" - and clattered away to fetch the never-changing venison and fried batter, with which, and Schicksalsee beer, the Frau Förster sustained her guests the year round, from "Georgi" to "Michaeli" and from "Michaeli" to "Georgi," reasoning that what she liked was good enough for them. The shapeless cook was ladling out dumplings, which she called "Nudel," into some soup for a Munich opera singer, who had just arrived by the stage. Anna confided to her that this was a "feiner Herr," and must be served accordingly. The kind Herr Förster came up to greet his guest. Mrs Dene introduced him as Mr Gethryn, of New York. At this Mr Blumenthal bounced forward from a corner where he had been spying and shook hands hilariously. "Vell! and how it goes!" he cried. Rex saw Ruth's face as she turned away, and stepping to her side, he whispered, "Friend of yours?" The teasing tone woke a thousand memories of their boy and girl days, and Ruth's young lady reserve had changed to the frank camaraderie of former times when she shook her head at him, laughing, as he looked back at them from the stairs, up which he was following Grethi and his portmanteau to the room prepared for him.

Half an hour later Mrs Dene and her daughter were looking with approval at Rex and his hearty enjoyment of the Frau Förster's fare. The cook, on learning that this was a "feiner Herr," had added trout to the regulation dishes; and although she was convinced that the only proper way to cook them was "blau gesotten" - meaning boiled to a livid bluish white - she had learned American tastes from the Denes and sent them in to Gethryn beautifully brown and crisp.

Rex turned one over critically. "Good little fish. Who is the angler?"

"Oh! angler! They were caught with bait," said Ruth, wrinkling her nose.

Rex gave her a quick look. "I suppose you have forgotten how to cast a fly."

"No, I think not," she answered quietly.

Mrs Dene opened her mouth to speak, and then discreetly closed it again in silence, reflecting that whatever there was to come on that point would get itself said without any assistance from her.

"I had a look at the water as I came along," continued Rex. "It seemed good casting."

"I never see it but I think how nice it would be to whip," said Ruth.

"No! really? Not outgrown the rod and fly since you grew into ball dresses?"

"Try me and see."

"Now, my dearest child! - "

"Yes, my dearest mother! - "

"Yes, dearest Mrs Dene! - "

"Oh! nonsense! listen to me, you children. Ruth danced herself ill at Cannes; and she lost her color, and she had a little cough, and she has it still, and she is very easily tired - "

"Only of not fishing and hunting, dearest, most perfect of mothers! You won't put up papa to forbid my going with him and Rex!"

"Your mother is incapable of such an action. How little you know her worth! She is only waiting to be assured that you are to have my greenheart, with a reel that spins fifty yards of silk. She shall have it, Mrs Dene."

"Is it as good as the hornbeam?" asked Ruth, smiling.

"The old hornbeam! do you remember that? I say, Ruth, you spoke of shooting. Really, can you still shoot?"

"Could I ever forget after such teaching?"

"Well, now, I call that a girl!" cried Rex, enthusiastically.

"Let us hope some people won't call it a hoyden!" said Mrs Dene, with the tender pride that made her faultfinding like a caress. "The idea of a girl carrying an absurd little breech-loading rifle all over Europe!"

"What! the one I had built for her?"

"I suppose so," said Mrs Dene, with a shade more of reserve.

"Miss Dene, you shall kill the first chamois that I see!"

"I fear, Mr Gethryn, the Duke Alfons Adalbert Maximilian in Baiern will have something to say about that!"

"Oh - h - h! Preserved?"

"Yes, indeed, preserved!"

"But they told me I might shoot on the Sonne-wendjoch."

"Ah! But that's in Tyrol, just across the line. You can see it from here. Austrian game laws aren't Bavarian game laws, sir!"

"How much of this country does your duke own?"

"Just half a dozen mountains, and half a dozen lakes, and half a hundred trout streams, with all the splendid forests belonging to them."

"Lucky duke! And is the game preserved in the whole region? Can't one get a shot?"

"One cannot even carry a gun without a permit."

Rex groaned. "And the trout - I suppose they are preserved, too?"

"Yes, but the Herr Förster has the right to fish and so have his guests. There are, however, conditions. The fish you take are not yours. You must buy as many of them as you want to keep, afterward. And they must be brought home alive - or as nearly alive as is consistent with being shut up in a close, round, green tin box, full of water which becomes tepid as it is carried along by a peasant boy in the heat. They usually die of suffocation. But to the German mind that is all right. It is only not right when one kills them instantly and lays them in a cool creel, on fresh wet ferns and moss."

"Nevertheless, I think we will dispense with the boy and the green box, in favor of the ferns and moss, assisted by a five franc piece or two."

"It isn't francs any more; you're not in France. It's marks here, you know."

"Well, I have the same faith in the corrupting power of marks as of francs, or lire, or shillings, or dollars."

"And I think you will find your confidence justified," said Mrs Dene, smiling.

"Mamma trying to be cynical!" said Ruth, teasingly. "Isn't she funny, Rex!"

A thoughtful look stole over her mother's face. "I can be terrible, too, sometimes - " she said in her little, clear, high soprano voice; and she gazed musingly at the edge of a letter, which just appeared above the table, and then sank out of sight in her lap.

"A letter from papa! It came with the stage! What does he say?"

"He says - several things; for one, he is coming back tomorrow instead of the next day."

"Delightful! But there is more?"

Mrs Dene's face became a cheerful blank. "Yes, there is more," she said. A pause.

"Mamma," began Ruth, "do you think Griffins desirable as mothers?"

"Very, for bad children!" Mrs Dene relapsed into a pleasant reverie. Ruth looked at her mother as a kitten does in a game of tag when the old cat has retired somewhere out of reach and sits up smiling through the barrier.

"You find her sadly changed!" she said to Gethryn, in that silvery, mocking tone which she had inherited from her mother.

"On the contrary, I find her the same adorable gossip she always was. Whatever is in that letter, she is simply dying to tell us all about it."

"Suppose we try not speaking, and see how long she can stand that?"

Rex laid his repeater on the table. Two pairs of laughing eyes watched the dear little old lady. At the end of three minutes she raised her own; blue, sweet, running over with fun and kindness.

"The colonel has a polite invitation from the duke for himself, and his party, to shoot on the Red Peak."

Thirteen

In July the sun is still an early riser, but long before he was up next day a succession of raps on the door woke Gethryn, and a voice outside inquired, "Are you going fishing with me today, you lazy beggar?"

"Colonel!" cried Rex, and springing up and throwing open the door, he threatened to mingle his pajamas with the natty tweeds waiting there in a loving embrace. The colonel backed away, twisting his white mustache. "How do, Reggy! Same boy, eh? Yes. I drove from Schicksalsee this morning."

"This morning? Wasn't it last night?" said Rex, looking at the shadows on the opposite mountain.

"And I am going to get some trout," continued the colonel, ignoring the interruption. "So's Daisy. See my new waterproof rig?"

"Beautiful! but - is it quite the thing to wear a flower in one's fishing coat?"

"I'm not aware - " began the other stiffly, but broke down, shook his seal ring at Rex, and walking over to the glass, rearranged the bit of wild hyacinth in his buttonhole with care.

"And now," he said, "Daisy and I will give you just three quarters of an hour." Rex sent a shower from the water basin across the room.

"Look out for those new waterproof clothes, Colonel."

"I'll take them out of harm's way," said the colonel, and disappeared.

Before the time had expired Rex stood under the beech tree with his rod case and his creel. The colonel sat reading a novel. Mrs Dene was pouring out coffee. Ruth was coming down a path which led from a low shed, the door of which stood wide open, suffering the early sunshine to fall on something that lay stretched along the floor. It was a stag, whose noble head and branching antlers would never toss in the sunshine again.

"Only think!" cried Ruth breathlessly, "Federl shot a stag of ten this morning at daybreak on the Red Peak, and he's frightened out of his wits, for only the duke has a right to do that. Federl mistook it for a stag of eight. And they're in the velvet, besides!" she added rather incoherently. " What luck! Poor Federl! I asked him if that meant strafen, and he said he guessed not, only zanken."

"What's `strafen' and what's `zanken,' Daisy?" asked the Colonel, pronouncing the latter like "z" in buzz.

Ruth went up to her father and took his face between her hands, dropping a light kiss on his eyebrow.

" Strafen is when one whips bad boys and t - s - zanken is when one only scolds them. Which shall we do to you, dear? Both?"

"We'll take coffee first, and then we'll see which there's time for before we leave you hemming a pocket handkerchief while Rex and I go trout fishing."

"Such parents!" sighed Ruth, nestling down beside her father and looking over her cup at Rex, who gravely nodded sympathy.

After breakfast, as Ruth stood waiting by the table where the fishing tackle lay, perfectly composed in manner, but unable to keep the color from her cheek and the sparkle of impatience from her eye, Gethryn thought he had seldom seen anything more charming.

A soft gray Tam crowned her pretty hair. A caped coat, fastened to the throat, hung over the short kilt skirt, and rough gaiters buttoned down over a wonderful little pair of hobnailed boots.

"I say! Ruth! what a stunner you are!" cried he with enthusiasm. She turned to the rod case and began lifting and arranging the rods.

"Rex," she said, looking up brightly, "I feel about sixteen today."

"Or less, judging from your costume," said her mother. "Schicksalsee isn't Rangely, you know. I only hope the good people in the little ducal court won't call you theatrical."

"A theatrical stunner!" mused Ruth, in her clearest tones. "It is good to know how one strikes one's friends."

"The disciplining of this young person is to be left to me," said the colonel. "Daisy, everything else about you is all wrong, but your frock is all right."

"That is simple and comprehensive and reassuring," murmured Ruth absently, as she bent over the fly-book with Gethryn.

After much consultation and many thoughtful glances at the bit of water which glittered and dashed through the narrow meadow in front of the house, they arranged the various colored lures and leaders, and standing up, looked at Colonel Dene, reading his novel.

"What? Oh! Come along, then!" said he, on being made aware that he was waited for, and standing up also, he dropped the volume into his creel and lighted a cigar.

"Are you going to take that trash along, dear?" asked his daughter.

"What trash? The work of fiction? That's literature, as the gentleman said about Dante."

"Rex," said Mrs Dene, buttoning the colonel's coat over his snowy collar, "I put this expedition into your hands. Take care of these two children."

She stood and watched them until they passed the turn beyond the bridge. Mr Blumenthal watched them too, from behind the curtains in his room. His leer went from one to the other, but always returned and rested on Rex. Then, as there was a mountain chill in the morning air, he crawled back into bed, hauling his night cap over his generous ears and rolling himself in a cocoon of featherbeds, until he should emerge about noon, like some sleek, fat moth.

The anglers walked briskly up the wooded road, chatting and laughing, with now and then a sage and critical glance at the water, of which they caught many glimpses through the trees. Gethryn and Ruth were soon far ahead. The colonel sauntered along, switching leaves with his rod and indulging in bursts of Parisian melody.

"Papa," called Ruth, looking back, "does your hip trouble you today, or are you only lazy?"

"Trot along, little girl; I'll be there before you are," said the colonel airily, and stopped to replace the wild hyacinth in his coat by a prim little pink and white daisy. Then he lighted a fresh cigar and started on, but their voices were already growing faint in the distance. Observing this, he stopped and looked up and down the road. No one was in sight. He sat down on the bank with his hand on his hip. His face changed from a frown to an expression of sharp pain. In five minutes he had grown from a fresh elderly man into an old man, his face drawn and gray, but he only muttered "the devil!" and sat still. A big bronze-winged beetle whizzed past him, z - z - ip! "like a bullet," he thought, and pressed both hands now on his hip. "Twenty-five years ago - pshaw! I'm not so old as that!" But it was twenty-five years ago when the blue-capped troopers, bursting in to the rescue, found the dandy " - th," scorched and rent and blackened, still reeling beneath a rag crowned with a gilt eagle. The exquisite befeathered and gold laced " - th." But the shells have rained for hours among the "Dandies" - and some are dead, and some are wishing for death, like that youngster lying there with the shattered hip.

Colonel Dene rose up presently and relighted his cigar; then he flicked some dust from the new tweeds, picked a stem of wild hyacinth, and began to whistle. "Pshaw! I'm not so old as all that!" he murmured, sauntering along the pleasant wood-road. Before long he came in sight of Ruth and Gethryn, who were waiting. But he only waved them on, laughing.

"Papa always says that old wound of his does not hurt him, but it does. I know it does," said Ruth.

Rex noted what tones of tenderness there were in her cool, clear voice. He did not answer, for he could only agree with her, and what could be the use of that?

They strolled on in silence, up the fragrant forest road. Great glittering dragonflies drifted along the river bank, or hung quivering above pools. Clouds of lazy sulphur butterflies swarmed and floated, eddying up from the road in front of them and settling down again in their wake like golden dust. A fox stole across the path, but Gethryn did not see him. The mesh of his landing net was caught just then in a little gold clasp that he wore on his breast.

"How quaint!" cried Ruth; "let me help you; there! One would think you were a French legitimist, with your fleur-de-lis."

"Thank you" - was all he answered, and turned away, as he felt the blood burn his face. But Ruth was walking lightly on and had not noticed. The fleur-de-lis, however, reminded her of something she had to say, and she began again, presently -

"You left Paris rather suddenly, did you not, Rex?"

This time he colored furiously, and Ruth, turning to him, saw it. She flushed too, fearing to have made she knew not what blunder, but she went on seriously, not pausing for his answer:

"The year before, that is three years ago now, we waited in Italy, as we had promised to do, for you to join us. But you never even wrote to say why you did not come. And you haven't explained it yet, Rex."

Gethryn grew pale. This was what he had been expecting. He knew it would have to come; in fact he had wished for nothing more than an opportunity for making all the amends that were possible under the circumstances. But the possible amends were very, very inadequate at best, and now that the opportunity was here, his courage failed, and he would have shirked it if he could. Besides, for the last five minutes, Ruth had been innocently stirring memories that made his heart beat heavily.

And now she was waiting for her answer. He glanced at the clear profile as she walked beside him. Her eyes were raised a little; they seemed to be idly following the windings of a path that went up the opposite mountainside; her lips rested one upon the other in quiet curves. He thought he had never seen such a pure, proud looking girl. All the chivalry of a generous and imaginative man brought him to her feet.

"I cannot explain. But I ask your forgiveness. Will you grant it? I won't forgive myself!"

She turned instantly and gave him her hand, not smiling, but her eyes were very gentle. They walked on a while in silence, then Rex said:

"Ever since I came, I have been trying to find courage to ask pardon for that unpardonable conduct, but when I looked in your dear mother's face, I felt myself such a brute that I was only fit to hold my tongue. And I believed," he added, after a pause, "that she would forgive me too. She was always better to me than I deserved."

"Yes," said Ruth.

"And you also are too good to me," he continued, "in giving me this chance to ask your pardon." His voice took on the old caressing tone in which he used to make peace after their boy and girl tiffs. "I knew very well that with you I should have a stricter account to settle than with your mother," he said, smiling.

"Yes," said Ruth again. And then with a little effort and a slight flush she added:

"I don't think it is good for men when too many excuses are made for them. Do you?"

"No, I do not," answered Rex, and thought, if all women were like this one, how much easier it would be for men to lead a good life! His heart stopped its heavy beating. The memories which he had been fighting for two years faded away once more; his spirits rose, and he felt like a boy as he kept step with Ruth along the path which had now turned and ran close beside the stream.

"Now tell me something of your travels," said Ruth. "You have been in the East."

"Yes, in Japan. But first I stopped a while in India with some British officers, nice fellows. There was some pheasant shooting."

"Pheasants! No tigers?"

"One tiger."

"You shot him! Oh! tell me about it!"

"No, I only saw him."

"Where?"

"In a jungle."

"Did you fire?"

"No, for he was already dead, and the odor which pervaded his resting place made me hurry away as fast as if he had been alive."

"You are a provoking boy!"

Rex laughed. "I did shoot a cheetah in China."

"A dead one?"

"No, he was snarling over a dead buck."

"Then you do deserve some respect."

"If you like. But it was very easy. One bullet settled

him. I was fined afterward."

"Fined! for what?"

"For shooting the Emperor's trained cheetah. After that I always looked to see if the game wore a silver collar before I fired."

Ruth would not look as if she heard.

Rex went on teasingly: "I assure you it was embarrassing, when the pheasants were bursting cover, to be under the necessity of inquiring at the nearest house if those were really pheasants or only Chinese hens."

"Rex," exclaimed Ruth, indignantly, "I hope you don't think I believe a word you are saying."

They had stopped to rest beside the stream, and now the colonel sauntered into view, his hands full of wild flowers, his single eyeglass gleaming beside his delicate straight nose.

"Do you know," he asked, strolling up to Ruth and tucking a cluster of bluebells under her chin, "do you know what old Hugh Montgomery would say if he were here?"

"He'd say," she replied promptly, "that `we couldn't take no traout with the pesky sun a shinin' and a brilin' the hull crick.'"

"Yes," said Rex. "Rise at four, east wind, cloudy morning, that was Hugh. But he could cast a fly."

"Couldn't he!" said the colonel. "`I cal'late ter chuck a bug ez fur ez enny o' them city fellers, 'n I kin,' says Hugh. Going to begin here, Rex?"

"What does Ruth think?"

"She thinks she isn't in command of this party," Ruth replied.

"It will take us until late in the afternoon to whip the stream from here to the lowest bridge." Rex smiled down at her and pushed back his cap with a boyish gesture.

She had forgotten it until that moment. Now it brought a perfect flood of pleasant associations. She had seen him look that way a hundred times when, in their teens, they two had lingered by the Northern Lakes. Her whole face changed and softened, but she turned away, nodding assent, and went and stood by her father, looking down at him with the bantering air which was a family trait. The lively colonel had found a sunny log on the bank, where he was sitting, leisurely joining his rod.

"Hello!" he cried, glancing up, "what are you two amateurs about? As usual, I'm ready to begin before Rex is awake!" and stepping to the edge he landed his flies with a flourish in a young birch tree. Rex came and disengaged them, and he received the assistance with perfect self-possession.

"Now see the new waterproof rig wade!" said Ruth, saucily.

"Go and wade yourself and don't bully your old

father!" cried the colonel.

"Old! this child old!"

"Oh! come along, Ruth!" called Rex, waiting on the shore and falling unconsciously into the tone of sixteen speaking to twelve.

For answer she slipped the cover from her slender rod and dexterously fitted the delicate tip to the second joint.

"Hasn't forgotten how to put a rod together! Wonderful girl!"

"Oh, I knew you were waiting to see me place the second joint in the butt first!" She deftly ran the silk through the guides, and then scientifically knotting the leader, slipped on a cast of three flies and picked her way daintily to the river bank. As she waded in the sudden cold made her gasp a little to herself, but she kept straight on without turning her head, and presently stepped on a broad, flat rock over which the water was slipping smoothly.

Gethryn waited near the bank and watched her as she sent the silk hissing thirty feet across the stream. The line swished and whistled, and the whole cast, hand fly, dropper and stretcher settled down lightly on the water. He noticed the easy motion of the wrist, the boyish pose of the slender figure, the serious sweet face, half shaded by the soft woolen Tam.

Swish - h - h! Swish - h - h! She slowly spun out forty feet, glancing back at Gethryn with a little laugh. Suddenly there was a tremendous splash, just beyond the dropper, answered by a turn of the white wrist, and then the reel fairly shrieked as the line melted away like a thread of smoke. Gethryn's eyes glittered with excitement, and the colonel took his cigar out of his mouth. But they didn't shout, "You have him! Go easy on him! Want any help!" They kept quiet.

Cautiously, and by degrees, Ruth laced her little gloved fingers over the flying line, and presently a quiver of the rod showed that the fish was checked. She reeled in, slowly and steadily for a moment, and then, whiz - z - z! off he dashed again. At seventy feet the rod trembled and the trout was still. Again and again she urged him toward the shore, meeting his furious dashes with perfect coolness and leading him dexterously away from rocks and roots. When he sulked she gave him the butt, and soon the full pressure sent him flying, only to end in a furious full length leap out of water, and another sulk.

The colonel's cigar went out.

At last she spoke, very quietly, without looking back.

"Rex, there is no good place to beach him here; will you net him, please?" Rex was only waiting for this; he had his landing net already unslung and he waded to her side.

"Now!" she whispered. The fiery side of a fish glittered just beneath the surface. With a skillful dip, a splash, and a spatter the trout lay quivering on the bank.

Gethryn quickly ended his life and held him up to view.

"Beautiful!" cried the colonel. "Good girl, Daisy! but don't spoil your frock!" And picking up his own rod he relighted his cigar and essayed some conscientious casting on his own account. But he soon wearied of the paths of virtue and presently went in search of a grasshopper, with evil intent.

Meanwhile Ruth was blushing to the tips of her ears at Gethryn's praises.

"I never saw a prettier sight!" he cried. "You're - you're splendid, Ruth! Nerve, judgment, skill - my dear girl, you have everything!"

Ruth's eyes shone like stars as she watched him in her turn while he sent his own flies spinning across a pool. And now there was nothing to be heard but the sharp whistle of the silk and the rush of the water. It seemed a long time that they had stood there, when suddenly the colonel created a commotion by hooking and hauling forth a trout of meagre proportions. Unheeding Rex's brutal remarks, he silently inspected his prize dangling at the end of the line. It fell back into the water and darted away gayly upstream, but the colonel was not in the least disconcerted and strolled off after another grasshopper.

"Papa! are you a bait fisherman!" cried his daughter severely.

The colonel dropped his hat guiltily over a lively young cricket, and standing up said "No!" very loud.

It was no use - Ruth had to laugh, and shortly afterward he was seated comfortably on the log again, his line floating with the stream, in his hands a volume with yellow paper covers, the worse for wear, bearing on its back the legend "Calman Levy, Editeur."

Rex soon struck a good trout and Ruth another, but the first one remained the largest, and finally Gethryn called to the colonel, "If you don't mind, we're going on."

"All right! take care of Daisy. We will meet and lunch at the first bridge." Then, examining his line and finding the cricket still there, he turned up his coat collar to keep off sunburn, opened his book, and knocked the ashes from his cigar.

"Here," said Gethryn two hours later, "is the bridge, but no colonel. Are you tired, Ruth? And hungry?"

"Yes, both, but happier than either!"

"Well, that was a big trout, the largest we shall take today, I think."

They reeled in their dripping lines, and sat down under a tree beside the lunch basket, which a boy from the lodge was guarding.

"I wish papa would come," said Ruth, with an anxious look up the road. "He ought to be hungry too, by this time."

Rex poured her a cup of red Tyroler wine and handed her a sandwich. Then, calling the boy, he gave him such a generous "Viertel" for himself as caused him to retire precipitately and consume it with grins, modified by boiled sausage. Ruth looked after him and smiled in sympathy. "I wonder how papa got rid of the other one with the green tin water-box."

"I know; I was present at the interview," laughed Rex. "Your father handed him a ten mark piece and said, `Go away, you superfluous Bavarian!'"

"In English?"

"Yes, and he must have understood, for he grinned and went."

It was good to hear the ring of Ruth's laugh. She was so happy that she found the smallest joke delightful, and her voice was very sweet. Rex lighted a cigarette and leaned back against a tree, in great comfort. Ruth, perched on a log, watched the smoke drift and curl. Gethryn watched her. They each cared as much for the hours they had spent in the brook, and for their wet clothing, as vigorous, happy, and imprudent youth ever cares about such things.

"So you are happy, Ruth?"

"Perfectly. And you? - But it takes more to make a spoiled young man happy than - "

"Than a spoiled young woman? I don't know about that. Yes, I - am - happy." Was the long puff of smoke ascending slowly responsible for the pauses between his words? A slight shadow was in his eyes for one moment. It passed, and he turned on her his most charming smile, as he repeated, "Perfectly happy!"

"Still no colonel!" he went on; "when he comes he will be tired. We don't want any more trout, do we? We have eighteen, all good ones. Suppose we rest and go

back all together by the road?" Ruth nodded, smiling to
see him fondle the creel full of shining fish, bedded on
fragrant leaves.

Rex's cap lay beside him, his head leaned back against
the tree, his face was turned up to the bending
branches. Presently he closed his eyes.

It might have been one minute, or ten. Ruth sat and
watched him. He had grown very handsome. He had
that pleasant air of good breeding which some men
retain under any and all circumstances. It has nothing
to do with character, and yet it is difficult to think ill of
a man who possesses it. When she had seen him last,
his nose was too near a snub to inspire much respect,
and his mustache was still in the state of colorless
scarcity. Now his hair and mustache were thick and
tawny, and his features were clear and firm. She
noticed the pleasant line of the cheek, the clean curve
of the chin, the light on the crisp edges of his close-cut
hair - the two freckles on his nose, and she decided that
that short, straight nose, with its generous and
humorous nostrils, was wholly fascinating. As girls
always will, she began to wonder about his life - idly at
first, but these speculations lead one sometimes farther
than one was prepared to go at the start. How much of
his delightful manner to them all was due to affection,
and how much to kindliness and good spirits? How
much did he care for those other friends, for that other
life in Paris? Who were the friends? What was the life?
She looked at him, it seemed to her, a long time. Had
he ever loved a woman? Was he still in love, perhaps,
with someone? Ruth was no child. But she was a lady,
and a proud one. There were things she did not choose
to think about, although she knew of their existence
well enough. She brought herself up at this point with a

Robert W. Chambers

sharp pull, and just then Gethryn, opening his eyes, smiled at her.

She turned quickly away; to her perfect consternation her cheeks grew hot. Bewildered by her own confusion, she rose as she turned, and saying how lovely the water looked, went and stood on the bridge, leaning over. Rex was on his feet in an instant, so covered with confusion too, that he never saw hers.

"I say, Ruth, I haven't been such a brute as to fall asleep! Indeed I haven't! I was thinking of Braith."

"And if you had fallen asleep you wouldn't be a brute, you tired boy! And who is Braith?"

Ruth turned smiling to meet him, restored to herself and thankful for the diversion.

"Braith," said Rex earnestly. "Braith is the best man in this wicked world, and my dearest friend. To whom," he added, "I have not written one word since I left him two ears ago."

Ruth's face fell. "Is that the way you treat your dearest friends?" - and she thought: "No wonder one is neglected when one is only an old playmate!" - but she was instantly ashamed of the little bitterness, and put it aside.

"Ah! you don't know of what we are capable," said Gethryn; and once more a shadow fell on his face.

A familiar form came jauntily down the road. Ruth hastened to meet it. "At last, Father! You want your luncheon, poor dear!"

"I do indeed, Daisy!"

The colonel came as gallantly up as if he had thirty pounds of trout to show instead of a creel that contained nothing but a novel by the newest and wickedest master of French fiction. He made a mild attempt to perjure himself about a large fish that had somehow got away from him, but desisted and merely added that a caning would be good for Rex.

Tired he certainly was, and when he was seated on the log and Ruth was bringing him his wine, he looked sharply at her and said, "You too, Daisy; you've done enough for the first day. We'll go home by the road."

"It is what I was just proposing to her," said Rex.

"Yes, you are both right," said Ruth. "I am tired."

"And happy?" laughed Rex. But perhaps Ruth did not hear, for she spoke at the same time to her father.

"Dear, you haven't told Rex yet how you got the invitation to shoot."

"Oh, yes! It was at an officers' dinner in Munich. The duke was there and I was introduced to him. He spoke of it as soon as they told him we were stopping here."

"He's a brick," said Rex, rising. "Shall we start for home, Colonel? Ruth must be tired."

When they turned in at the Forester's door, the colonel ordered Daisy to her room, where Mrs Dene and their maid were waiting to make her luxuriously comfortable with dry things, and rugs, and couches, and cups

Robert W. Chambers

of tea that were certainly not drawn from the Frau Förster's stores. Tea in Germany being more awful than tobacco, or tobacco more awful than tea, according as one cares most for tea or tobacco.

The colonel and Rex sat after supper under the big beech tree. Ruth, from her window, could see their cigars alight, and, now and then, hear their voices.

Rex was telling the colonel about Braith, of whom he had not ceased thinking since the afternoon. He went to his room early and wrote a long letter to him.

It began: "You did not expect to hear from me until I was cured. Well, you are hearing from me now, are you not?"

And it ended: "Only a few more weeks, and then I shall return to you and Paris, and the dear old life. This is the middle of July. In September I shall come back."

Fourteen

After the colonel's return, Mr Blumenthal found many difficulties in the way of that social ease which was his ideal. The ladies were never to be met with unaccompanied by the colonel or Gethryn; usually both were in attendance. If he spoke to Mrs Dene, or Ruth, it was always the colonel who answered, and there was a gleam in that trim warrior's single eyeglass which did not harmonize with the grave politeness of his voice and manner.

Rex had never taken Mr Blumenthal so seriously. He called him "Our Bowery brother," and "the Gentleman from West Brighton," and he passed some delightful moments in observing his gruesome familiarity with the maids, his patronage of the grave Jaegers, and his fraternal attitude toward the head of the house. It was great to see him hook a heavy arm in an arm of the tall, military Herr Förster, and to see the latter drop it.

But there came an end to Rex's patience.

One morning, when they were sitting over their coffee out of doors, Mr Blumenthal walked into their midst. He wore an old flannel shirt, and trousers too tight for him, inadequately held up by a strap. He displayed a tin bait box and a red and green float, and said he had come to inquire of Rex "vere to dig a leetle vorms," and also to borrow of him "dot feeshpole mitn seelbern ringes."

The request, and the grossness of his appearance before the ladies, were too much for a gentleman and an angler.

Rex felt his gorge rise, and standing up brusquely, he walked away. Ruth thoughtlessly slipped after him and murmured over his shoulder:

"Friend of yours?"

Gethryn's fists unclenched and came out of his pockets and he and Ruth went away together, laughing under the trees.

Mr Blumenthal stood where Rex had left him, holding out the bait-box and gazing after them. Then he turned and looked at the colonel and his wife. Perspiration glistened on his pasty, pale face and the rolls of fat that crowded over his flannel collar. His little, dead, white-rimmed, pale gray eyes had the ferocity of a hog's which has found something to rend and devour. He looked into their shocked faces and made a bow.

"Goot ma - a - rnin, Mister and Missess Dene!" he said, and turned his back.

The elderly couple exchanged glances as he disappeared.

"We won't mention this to the children," said the gentle old lady.

That was the last they saw of him. Nobody knew where he kept himself in the interval, but about a week later he came running down with a valise in his hand and jumped into a carriage from the "Green Bear" at Schicksalsee, which had just brought some people out and was returning empty. He forgot to give the usual "Trinkgeld" to the servants, and a lively search in his room discovered nothing but a broken collar button and a crumpled telegram in French. But Grethi had her compensation that evening, when she led the conversation in the kitchen and Mr Blumenthal was discussed in several South German dialects.

By this time August was well advanced, but there had been as yet no "Jagd-partie," as Sepp called the hunting excursion planned with such enthusiasm weeks before. After that first day in the trout stream, Ruth not only suffered more from fatigue than she had expected, but the little cough came back, causing her parents to draw the lines of discipline very tight indeed.

Ruth, whose character seemed made of equal parts of good taste and reasonableness, sweet temper and humor, did not offer the least opposition to discipline, and when her mother remarked that, after all, there was a difference between a schoolgirl and a young lady, she did not deny it. The colonel and Rex went off once or twice with the Jaegers, but in a halfhearted way, bringing back more experience than game. Then Rex went on a sketching tour. Then the colonel was suddenly called again to Munich to meet some old army men just arrived from home, and so it was not until about a week after Mr Blumenthal's departure that, one evening when the Sennerins were calling the cows on the upper Alm, a party of climbers came up the side of the Red Peak and stopped at

"Nani's Hütterl."

Sepp threw down the green sack from his shoulders to the bench before the door and shouted:

"Nani! du! Nani!" No answer.

"Mari und Josef!" he muttered; then raising his voice, again he called for Nani with all his lungs.

A muffled answer came from somewhere around the other side of the house. "Ja! komm glei!" And then there was nothing to do but sit on the bench and watch the sunset fade from peak to peak while they waited.

Nani did not come "glei" - but she came pretty soon, bringing with her two brimming milk-pails as an excuse for the delay.

She and Sepp engaged at once in a conversation, to which the colonel listened with feelings that finally had to seek expression.

"I believe," he said in a low voice, "that German is the language of the devil."

"I fancy he's master of more than one. And besides, this isn't German, any more than our mountain dialects are English. And really," Ruth went on, "if it comes to comparing dialects, it seems to me ours can't stand the test. These are harsh enough. But where in the world is human speech so ugly, so poverty-stricken, so barren of meaning and feeling, and shade and color and suggestiveness, as the awful talk of our rustics? A Bavarian, a Tyroler, often speaks a whole poem in a single word, like - "

"Do you think one of those poems is being spoken about our supper now, Daisy?"

"Sybarite!" cried Ruth, with that tinkle of fun in her voice which was always sounding between her and her parents; "I won't tell you." The truth was she did not dare to tell her hungry companions that, so far as she had been able to understand Sepp and Nani, their conversation had turned entirely on a platform dance - which they called a "Schuh-plattl" - and which they proposed to attend together on the following Sunday.

But Sepp, having had his gossip like a true South German hunter-man, finally did ask the important question:

"Ach! supper! du lieber Himmel!" There was little enough of that for the Herrschaften. There was black bread and milk, and there were some Semmel, but those were very old and hard.

"No cheese?"

"Nein!"

"No butter?"

"Nein!"

"Coffee?"

"Yes, but no sugar."

"Herr Je!"

When Sepp delivered this news to his party they all

laughed and said black bread and milk would do. So Nani invited them into her only room - the rest of the "Hütterl" was kitchen and cow-shed - and brought the feast.

A second Sennerin came with her this time, in a costume which might have startled them, if they had not already seen others like it. It consisted of a pair of high blue cotton trousers drawn over her skirts, the latter bulging all round inside the jeans. She had no teeth and there was a large goiter on her neck.

"Good Heavens!" muttered the colonel, setting down his bowl of milk and twisting around to stare out of the window behind him.

"Poor thing! she can't help it!" murmured Ruth.

"No more she can, you dear, good girl!" said Rex, and his eyes shone very kindly. Ruth caught her breath at the sudden beating of her heart.

What was left of daylight came through the little window and fell upon her face; it was as white as a flower, and very quiet.

Dusk was setting in when Sepp made his appearance. He stood about in some hesitation, and finally addressed himself to Ruth as the one who could best understand his dialect. She listened and then turned to her father.

"Sepp doesn't exactly know where to lodge me. He had thought I could stay here with Nani - "

"Not if I can help it!" cried the colonel.

"While," Ruth went on - "while you and Rex went up to the Jaeger's hut above there on the rocks. He says it's very rough at the Jagd-hütte."

"Is anyone else there? What does Sepp mean by telling us now for the first time? " demanded the colonel sharply.

"He says he was afraid I wouldn't come if I knew how rough it was - and that - " added Ruth, laughing - "he says would have been such a pity! Besides, he thought Nani was alone - and I could have had her room while she slept on the hay in the loft. I'm sure this is as neat as a mountain shelter could be," said Ruth - looking about her at the high piled feather beds, covered in clean blue and white check, and the spotless floor and the snow white pine table. "I'd like to stay here, only the - the other lady has just arrived too!"

"The lady in the blue overalls?"

"Yes - and - " Ruth stopped, unwilling to say how little relish she felt for the society of the second Sennerin. But Rex and her father were on their feet and speaking together.

"We will go and see about the Jagd-hütte. You don't mind being left for five minutes?"

"The idea! go along, you silly boys!"

The colonel came back very soon, and in the best of spirits.

"It's all right, Daisy! It's a dream of luxury!" and carried her off, hardly giving her time to thank Nani and to say a winningly kind word to the hideous one, who gazed back at her, pitchfork in hand, without reply. No one will ever know whether or not she felt any more cheered by Ruth's pleasant ways than the cows did who were putting their heads out from the stalls where she was working.

The dream of luxury was a low hut of two rooms. The outer one had a pile of fresh hay in one corner and a few blankets. Some of the dogs were already curled up there. The inner room contained two large bunks with hay and rugs and blankets; a bench ran where the bunks were not, around the sides; a shelf was above the bunks; there was a cupboard and a chest and a table.

"Why, this is luxury!" cried Ruth.

"Well - I think so, too. I'm immensely relieved. Sepp says artists bring their wives up here to stay over for the sunrise. You'll do? Eh?"

"I should think so!"

"Good! then Rex and I and Sepp and the Dachl" - he always would say "Dockles" - "will keep guard outside against any wild cows that may happen to break loose from Nani. Good night, little girl! Sure you're not too tired?"

Rex stood hesitating in the open door. Ruth went and gave him her hand. He kissed it, and she, meaning to please him with the language she knew he liked best, said, smiling, "Bonne nuit, mon ami!" At the same moment her father passed her, and the two men closed the door and went away together. The last glimmer of dusk was in the room. Ruth had not seen

Gethryn's face.

"Bonne nuit, mon ami!" Those tender, half forgotten - no! never, never forgotten words! Rex threw himself on the hay and lay still, his hands clenched over his breast.

The kindly colonel was sound asleep when Sepp came in with a tired but wagging hound, from heaven knows what scramble among the higher cliffs by starlight. The night air was chilly. Rex called the dog to his side and took him in his arms. "We will keep each other warm," he said, thinking of the pups. And Zimbach, assenting with sentimental whines, was soon asleep. But Gethryn had not closed his eyes when the Jaeger sprang up as the day broke. A faint gray light came in at the little window. All the dogs were leaping about the room. Sepp gave himself a shake, and his toilet was made.

"Colonel," said Rex, standing over a bundle of rugs and hay in which no head was visible, "Colonel! Sepp says we must hurry if we want to see a `gams.'"

The colonel turned over. What he said was: "Damn the Gomps!" But he thought better of that and stood up, looking cynical.

"Come and have a dip in the spring," laughed Rex.

When they took their dripping heads out of the wooden trough into which a mountain spring was pouring and running out again, leaving it always full, and gazed at life - between rubs of the hard crash towel - it had assumed a kinder aspect.

Half an hour later, when they all were starting for the

top, Ruth let the others pass her, and pausing for a moment with her hand on the lintel, she looked back into the little smoke-blackened hut. The door of the inner room was open. She had dreamed the sweetest dream of her life there.

Before the others could miss her she was beside them, and soon was springing along in advance, swinging her alpenstock. It seemed as if she had the wings as well as the voice of a bird.

> Der Jaeger zieht in grünem Wald
> Mit frölichem Halloh!

she sang.

Sepp laughed from the tip of his feather to the tip of his beard.

"Wie's gnädige Fraulein hat G'müth!" he said to Rex.

"What's that?" asked the colonel.

"He says," translated Rex freely, "What a lot of every delightful quality Ruth possesses!"

But Ruth heard, and turned about and was very severe with him. "Such shirking! Translate me Gemüth at once, sir, if you please!"

"Old Wiseboy at Yarvard confessed he couldn't, short of a treatise, and who am I to tackle what beats Wiseboy?"

"Can you, Daisy?" asked her father.

"Not in the least, but that's no reason for letting Rex off." Her voice took on a little of the pretty bantering tone she used to her parents. She was beginning to feel such a happy confidence in Rex's presence.

They were in the forest now, moving lightly over the wet, springy leaves, probing cautiously for dangerous, loose boulders and treacherous slides. When they emerged, it was upon a narrow plateau; the rugged limestone rocks rose on one side, the precipice plunged down on the other. Against the rocks lay patches of snow, grimy with dirt and pebbles; from a cleft the long greenish white threads of "Peter's beard" waved at them; in a hollow bloomed a thicket of pink Alpen-rosen.

They had just reached a clump of low firs, around the corner of a huge rock, when a rush of loose stones and a dull sound of galloping made them stop. Sepp dropped on his face; the others followed his example. The hound whined and pulled at the leash.

On the opposite slope some twenty Hirsch-cows, with their fawns, were galloping down into the valley, carrying with them a torrent of earth and gravel. Presently they slackened and stopped, huddling all together into a thicket. The Jaeger lifted his head and whispered "Stück"; that being the complimentary name by which one designates female deer in German.

"All?" said Rex, under his breath. At the same moment Ruth touched his shoulder.

On the crest of the second ridge, only a hundred yards distant, stood a stag, towering in black outline, the sun just coming up behind him. Then two other pairs of antlers rose from behind the ridge, two more stags lifted their heads and shoulders and all three stood silhouetted against the sky. They tossed and stamped and stared straight at the spot where their enemies lay hidden.

A moment, and the old stag disappeared; the others followed him.

"If they come again, shoot," said Sepp.

Rex passed his rifle to Ruth. They waited a few minutes; then the colonel jumped up.

"I thought we were after chamois!" he grumbled.

"So we are," said Rex, getting on his feet.

A shot rang out, followed by another. They turned, sharply. Ruth, looking half frightened, was lowering the smoking rifle from her shoulder. Across the ravine a large stag was swaying on the edge; then he fell and rolled to the bottom. The hound, loosed, was off like an arrow, scrambling and tumbling down the side. The four hunters followed, somehow. Sepp got down first and sent back a wild Jodel. The stag lay there, dead, and his splendid antlers bore eight prongs.

When Ruth came up she had her hand on her father's arm. She stood and leaned on him, looking down at the stag. Pity mingled with a wild intoxicating sense of achievement confused her. A rich color flushed her cheek, but the curve of her lips was almost grave.

Sepp solemnly drew forth his flask of Schnapps and, taking off his hat to her, drank "Waidmann's Heil!" - a toast only drunk by hunters to hunters.

Gethryn shook hands with her twenty times and praised her until she could bear no more.

She took her hand from her father's arm and drew herself up, determined to preserve her composure. The wind blew the little bright rings of hair across her crimson cheek and wrapped her kilts about her slender figure as she stood, her rifle poised across her shoulder, one hand on the stock and one clasped below the muzzle.

"Are you laughing at me, Rex?"

"You know I am not!"

Never had she been so happy in her whole life.

The game drawn and hung, to be fetched later, they resumed their climb and hastened upward toward the peak.

Ruth led. She hardly felt the ground beneath her, but sprang from rock to moss and from boulder to boulder, till a gasp from Gethryn made her stop and turn about.

"Good Heavens, Ruth! what a climber you are!"

And now the colonel sat down on the nearest stone and flatly refused to stir.

"Oh! is it the hip, Father?" cried Ruth, hurrying back and kneeling beside him.

"No, of course it isn't! It's indignation!" said her father, calmly regarding her anxious face. "If you can't go up mountains like a human girl, you're not going up any more mountains with me."

"Oh! I'll go like a human snail if you want, dear! I've been too selfish! It's a shame to tire you so!"

"Indeed, it is a perfect shame!" cried the colonel.

Ruth had to laugh. "As I remarked to Rex, early this morning," her father continued, adjusting his eyeglass, "hang the Gomps!" Rex discreetly offered no comment. "Moreover," the colonel went on, bringing all the severity his eyeglass permitted to bear on them both, "I decline to go walking any longer with a pair of lunatics. I shall confide you both to Sepp and will wait for you at the upper Shelter."

"But it's only indignation; it isn't the hip, Father?" said Ruth, still hanging about him, but trying to laugh, since he would have her laugh.

He saw her trouble, and changing his tone said seriously, "My little girl, I'm only tired of this scramble, that's all."

She had to be contented with this, and they separated, her father taking a path which led to the right, up a steep but well cleared ascent to a plateau, from which they could see the gable of a roof rising, and beyond that the tip-top rock with its white cross marking the highest point. The others passed to the left, around and among huge rocks, where all the hollows were full of grimy snow. The ground was destitute of trees and all shrubs taller than the hardy Alpen-rosen. Masses of rock lay piled about the limestone crags that formed the summit. The sun had not yet tipped their peak with purple and orange, but some of the others were lighting up. No insects darted about them; there was not a living thing among the near rocks except the bluish black salamanders, which lay here and there, cold and motionless.

They walked on in silence; the trail grew muddy, the ground was beaten and hatched up with small, sharp hoof prints. Sepp kneeled down and examined them.

"Hirsch, Reh, and fawn, and ja! ja! Sehen Sie? Gams!"

After this they went on cautiously. All at once a peculiar shrill hiss, half whistle, half cry, sounded very near.

A chamois, followed by two kids, flashed across a heap of rocks above their heads and disappeared. The Jaeger muttered something, deep in his beard.

"You wouldn't have shot her?" said Ruth, timidly.

"No, but she will clear this place of chamois. It's useless to stay here now."

It was an hour's hard pull to the next peak. When at last they lay sheltered under a ledge, grimy snow all about them, the Jaeger handed his glass to Ruth.

"Hirsch on the Kaiser Alm, three Reh by Nani's Hütterl, and one in the ravine," he said, looking at Gethryn, who was searching eagerly with his own glass. Ruth balanced the one she held against her alpenstock.

"Yes, I see them all - and - why, there's a chamois!"

Sepp seized the glass which she held toward him.

"The gracious Fraülein has a hunter's eyesight; a chamois is feeding just above the Hirsch."

"We are right for the wind, but is this the best place?" said Rex.

"We must make the best of it," said Sepp.

The speck of yellow was almost imperceptibly approaching their knoll, but so slowly that Ruth almost doubted if it moved at all.

Sepp had the glass, and declining the one Rex offered her, she turned for a moment to the superb panorama at their feet. East, west, north and south the mountain world extended. By this time the snow mountains of Tyrol were all lighted to gold and purple, rose and faintest violet. Sunshine lay warm now on all the near peaks. But great billowy oceans of mist rolled below along the courses of the Alp-fed streams, and, deep under a pall of heavy, pale gray cloud, the Trauerbach was rushing through its hidden valley down to Schicksalsee and Todtstein. There was perfect silence, only now and then made audible by the tinkle of a distant cowbell and the Jodel of a Sennerin. Ruth turned again toward the chamois. She could see it now without a glass. But Sepp placed his in her hand.

The chamois was feeding on the edge of a cliff, moving here and there, leaping lightly across some gully, tossing its head up for a precautionary sniff. Suddenly it gave a bound and stood still, alert. Two great clumsy "Hirsch-kühe" had taken fright at some imaginary danger, and, uttering their peculiar half grunt, half roar, were galloping across the alm in half real, half assumed panic with their calves at their heels.

The elderly female Hirsch is like a timorous granny who loves to scare herself with ghost stories, and adores the sensation of jumping into bed before the robber under it can catch her by the ankle.

It was such an alarm as this which now sent the two fussy old deer, with their awkward long legged calves, clattering away with terror-stricken roars which startled the delicate chamois, and for one moment petrified him. The next, with a bound, he fairly flew along the crest, seeming to sail across the ravine like a hawk, and to cover distances in the flash of an eye. Sepp uttered a sudden exclamation and forgot everything but what he saw. He threw his rifle forward, there was a sharp click! - the cartridge had not exploded. Next moment he remembered himself and turned ashamed and deprecating to Gethryn. The latter laid his hand on the Jaeger's arm and pointed. The chamois' sharp ear had caught the click! - he swerved aside and bounded to a point of rock to look for this new danger. Rex tried to put his rifle in Ruth's hands. She pressed it back, resolutely. "It is your turn," she motioned with her lips, and drew away out of his reach. That was no time for argument. The Jaeger nodded, "Quick!" A shot echoed among the rocks and the chamois disappeared.

"Is he hit? Oh, Rex! did you hit him?"

"Ei! Zimbach!" Sepp slipped the leash, the hound sprang away, and in a moment his bell-like voice announced Rex's good fortune.

Ruth flew like the wind, not heeding their anxious calls to be careful, to wait for help. It was not far to go, and her light, sure foot brought her to the spot first. When Rex and Sepp arrived she was kneeling beside the dead chamois, stroking the "beard" that waved along its bushy spine. She sprang up and held out her hand to Gethryn.

"Look at that beard - Nimrod!" she said. Her voice rang with an excitement she had not shown at her own success.

"It is a fine beard," said Rex, bending over it. His voice was not quite steady. "Herrlich!" cried Sepp, and drank the "Waidmann's Heil!" toast to him in deep and serious draughts. Then he took out a thong, tied the four slender hoofs together and opened his game sack; Rex helped him to hoist the chamois in and onto his broad shoulders.

Now for the upper Shelter. They started in great spirits, a happy trio. Rex was touched by Ruth's deep delight in his success, and by the pride in him which she showed more than she knew. He looked at her with eyes full of affection. Sepp was assuring himself, by all the saints in the Bavarian Calendar, that here was a "Herrschaft" which a man might be proud of guiding, and so he meant to tell the duke. Ruth's generous heart beat high.

Their way back to the path where they had separated from Colonel Dene was long and toilsome. Sepp did his best to beguile it with hunter's yarns, more or less true, at any rate just as acceptable as if they had been proved and sworn to.

Like a good South German he hated Prussia and all its works, and his tales were mostly of Berliners who had wandered thither and been abused; of the gentleman who had been told, and believed, that the "gams" slept by hooking its horns into crevices of the rock, swinging thus at ease, over precipices; of another whom Federl once deterred from going on the mountains by telling how a chamois, if enraged, charged and butted; of a third who went home glad to have learned that the chamois produced their peculiar call by bringing up a hind leg and whistling through the hoof.

It was about half past two in the afternoon and Ruth began to be very, very tired, when a Jodel from Sepp greeted the "Hütte" and the white cross rising behind it. As they toiled up the steep path to the little alm, Ruth said, "I don't see Papa, but there are people there." A man in a summer helmet, wound with a green veil, came to the edge of the wooden platform and looked down at them; he was presently joined by two ladies, of whom one disappeared almost immediately, but they could see the other still looking down until a turn in the path brought them to the bottom of some wooden steps, close under the platform. On climbing these they were met at the top by the gentleman, hat in hand, who spoke in French to Gethryn, while the stout, friendly lady held out both hands to Ruth and cried, in pretty broken English:

"Ah! dear Mademoiselle! ees eet possible zat we meet a - h - gain!"

"Madame Bordier!" exclaimed Ruth, and kissed her

cordially on both cheeks. Then she greeted the husband of Madame, and presented Rex.

"But we know heem!" smiled Madame; and her quiet, gentlemanly husband added in French that Monsieur the colonel had done them the honor to leave messages with them for Miss Dene and Mr Gethryn.

"Papa is not here?" said Ruth, quickly.

Monsieur the colonel, finding himself a little fatigued, had gone on to the Jaeger-hütte, where were better accommodations.

Ruth's face fell, and she lost her bright color.

"But no! my dear!" said Madame. "Zere ees nossing ze mattaire. Your fazzer ees quite vell," and she hurried her indoors.

Rex and Monsieur Bordier were left together on the platform. The amiable Frenchman did the honors as if it were a private salon. Monsieur the colonel was perfectly well. But perfectly! It was really for Mademoiselle that he had gone on. He had decided that it would be quite too fatiguing for his daughter to return that day to Trauerbach, as they had planned, and he had gone on to secure the Jagd-hütte for the night before any other party should arrive.

"He watched for you until you turned into the path that leads up here, and we all saw that you were quite safe. It is only half an hour since he left. He did us the honor to say that Mademoiselle Dene could need no better chaperon than my wife - Monsieur the colonel was a little fatigued, but badly, no."

Monsieur Bordier led the way to the usual spring and wooden trough behind the house, and, while Rex was enjoying a refreshing dip, he continued to chat.

Yes, as he had already had the honor to inform Rex, Mademoiselle had been his wife's pupil in singing, the last two winters, in Paris. Monsieur Gethryn, perhaps, was not wholly unacquainted with the name of Madame Bordier?

"Madame's reputation as an artist, and a professor of singing, is worldwide," said Rex in his best Parisian, adding:

"And you, then, Monsieur, are the celebrated manager of `La Fauvette'?"

The manager replied with a politely gratified bow.

"The most charming theater in Paris," added Rex.

"Ah! murmured the other, Monsieur is himself an artist, though not of our sort, and artists know."

"Colonel Dene has told you that I am studying in Paris," said Rex modestly.

"He has told me that Monsieur exhibited in the salon with a number one."

Rex scrubbed his brown and rosy cheeks with the big towel.

Monsieur Bordier went on: "But the talent of Mademoiselle! Mon Dieu! what a talent! What a voice of silver and crystal! And today she will meet another pupil of Madame - of ours - a genius. My word!"

"Today?"

"Yes, she is with us here. She makes her debut at the Fauvette next autumn."

Rex concealed a frown in the ample folds of the towel. It crossed his mind that the colonel might better have stayed and taken care of his own daughter. If he, Rex, had had a sister, would he have liked her to be on a Bavarian mountaintop in a company composed of a gamekeeper, the manager of a Paris theater and his wife, and a young person who was about to make her debut in opera-bouffe, and to have no better guardian than a roving young art student? Rex felt his unfitness for the post with a pang of compunction. Meantime he rubbed his head, and Monsieur Bordier talked tranquilly on. But between vexation and friction Gethryn lost the thread of Monsieur's remarks for a while.

The first word which recalled his wandering attention was "Chamois?" and he saw that Monsieur Bordier was pointing to the game bag and looking amiably at Sepp, who, divided between sulkiness at Monsieur's native language and goodwill toward anyone who seemed to be accepted by his "Herrschaften," was in two minds whether to open the bag and show the game to this smiling Frenchman, or "to say him a Grobheit" and go away. Sepp's "Grobheit" could be very insulting indeed when he cared to make it so. Rex hastened to turn the scale.

"Yes, Herr Director, this is Sepp, one of the duke's best gamekeepers - Monsieur speaks German?" he interrupted himself to ask in French.

"Parfaitement! Well," he went on in Sepp's native tongue, "Herr Director, in Sepp you see one of the best woodsmen in Bavaria, one of the best shots in Germany. Sepp, we must show the Herr Director our Gems."

And there was nothing for Sepp but to open the bag, sheepish, beaten, laughing in spite of himself, and before he knew it they all three had their heads together over the game in perfect amity.

A step sounded along the front platform, and Madame looked round the corner of the house, saying that lunch was ready. Her husband and Rex joined her immediately. "Ze young ladees are wizin," she said, and led the way.

The sun-glare on the limestone rocks outside made the little room seem almost black at first, and all Rex could distinguish as he followed the others was Ruth's bright smile as she stood near the door and a jumble of dark figures farther back.

"Permit me," said Monsieur, "to introduce you to our Belle Hélène." Rex had already bowed low, seeing nothing. "Mademoiselle Descartes - Monsieur Gethryn - " Rex raised his head and looked into the white face of Yvonne.

"Ah, yes! as I was saying," gossiped Monsieur while they were taking their places at table, "I shoot when I can, but merely the partridge and rabbit of the turnip. Bah! a man may not boast of that!"

Rex kept his eyes fixed on the speaker and forced himself to understand what was being said.

"But the sanglier?" His voice sounded in his ears like noises one hears with the head under water.

"Mon Dieu! the sanglier! yes, that is also noble game. I do not deny it." Monsieur talked on evenly and quietly in his self-possessed, reasonable voice, about the habits and the hunt of the wild boar.

Ruth, sitting opposite, forcing herself to swallow the food, to answer Madame gaily and look at her ease, felt her heart settle down like lead in her breast.

What was this? Oh! what was it? She looked at Mademoiselle Descartes. This young, gentle stranger with the dark hair and the face like marble, this girl whom she had never heard of until an hour ago, was hiding from Rex behind the broad shoulders of Madame Bordier. The pupils of her blue eyes were so dilated that the sad, frightened eyes themselves looked black. Ruth turned to Gethryn. He was listening and answering. About his nostrils and temples the hollows showed; the flush of sunburn was gone, leaving only a pallid brown over the ashen grey of his face; his expression varied between a strained smile and a fixed stare. The cold weight at her heart melted and swelled in a passion of pity.

"Someone must keep up! Someone must keep up!" she said to herself; and turned to assure Madame in tones which deserved the name of "crystal and silver," that, Yes, for her part she had not been able to see any reason why hearing Parsifal at Bayreuth should make one forget that Bizet was also a great master.

But the strain became too great, and at the first possible moment she said brightly to Rex, "I'm going to feed Zimbach. Sepp said I might." She collected some scraps on a plate and went out. The hound rose wagging as she approached. Ruth stood a moment looking down at him. Then she knelt and took his brown head in her arms. Her eyes were full of tears. Zimbach licked her face, and then wrenching his head away began to dance about her, barking and running at the platter. She took a bone and gave it to him; it went with a snap; so bit by bit she fed him with her own hands, and the tears dried without one falling.

She heard Rex come out and stood up to meet him with clear grey eyes that seemed to see nothing but a jest.

"Look at this dog, Rex! He hasn't a word to say about the bones he's eaten already; he merely remarks that there don't seem to be any more at present!"

Rex was taking down his gun. "Monsieur wants to see this," he said in a dull, heavy voice. "And Ruth - when you are ready - your father, perhaps - "

"Yes, I really would like to join him as soon as possible - " They went in together.

An hour later they were taking leave. All the usual explanations had been made; everyone knew where the others were stopping, and why they were there, and how long they meant to stay, and where they intended to go afterward.

The Bordiers, with Yvonne, were at a lake on the opposite side of the mountain, but a visit to the Forester's house at Trauerbach was one of the excursions they had already planned.

It only remained now, as Ruth said, to fix upon an early day for coming.

The hour just past had been Ruth's hour.

Without effort, or apparent intention, she had taken and kept the lead from the moment when she returned with Rex. She it was who had given the key, who had set and kept the pitch, and it was due to her that not one discordant note had been struck. Vaguely yet vividly she felt the emergency. Refusing to ask herself the cause, she recognized a crisis. Something was dreadfully wrong. She made no attempt to go beyond that. Of all the deep emotions which she was learning now so suddenly, for the first time, the dominant one with her at present was a desire to help and to protect. All her social experience, all her tact, were needed to shield Rex and this white-faced, silent stranger, who, without her, must have betrayed themselves, so stunned, so dazed they were. And the courage of her father's daughter kept her fair head erect above the dead weight at her heart.

And now, having said "Au revoir" to Monsieur and Madame, and fixed upon a day for their visit to the Försthaus, she turned to Yvonne and took her hand.

"Mademoiselle, I regret so much to hear that you are not quite strong. But when you come to Trauerbach, Mama and I will take such good care of you that you will not mind the fatigue."

The sad blue eyes looked into the clear grey ones, and once more Ruth responded with a passion of grief and pity.

How Rex made his adieux Ruth never knew.

When he overtook her, she and Sepp were well started down the path to the Jagd-hütte. They seemed to be having a duet of silence, which Rex turned into a trio when he joined them.

For such walkers as they all were the distance they had to go was nothing. Soft afternoon lights were still lying peacefully beside the long afternoon shadows as they approached the little hut, and Sepp answered the colonel's abortive attempt at a Jodel with one so long and complicated that it seemed as if he were taking that means to express all he should have liked to say in words. The spell broken, he turned about and asked:

"Also! what did the French people," - he wouldn't call them Herrschaft - "say to the gracious Fraulein's splendid shot?"

Ruth stopped and looked absently at him, then flushed and recovered herself quickly. It was the first time she had remembered her stag.

"I fear," said she, "that French people would disapprove a young lady's shooting. I did not tell them."

Sepp went on again with long strides. The four little black hoofs of the chamois stuck pitifully up out of the bag on his broad back. When he was well out of hearing he growled aloud:

"Hab' 's schon g' wusst! Jesses, Marie and Josef! was is denn dös!"

That evening, when Rex and the Jaeger were fussing over the chamois' beard and dainty horns inside the Hütte, Ruth and her father stood without, before the closed door. The skies were almost black, and full of stars. Through the wide fragrant stillness came up now and then a Jodel from some Bursch going to visit his Sennerin. A stamp, and a comfortable sigh, came at times from Nani's cows in their stall below.

Ruth put both arms around her father's neck and laid her head down on his shoulder.

"Tired, Daisy?"

"Yes, dear."

Fifteen

Supper was over, evening had fallen; but there would be no music tonight under the beech tree; the sky was obscured by clouds and a wet wind was blowing.

Mrs Dene and Ruth were crossing the hall; Gethryn came in at the front door and they met.

"Well?" said Rex, forcing a smile.

"Well," said Ruth. "Mademoiselle Descartes is better. Madame will bring her down stairs by and by. It appears that wretched peasant who drove them has been carrying them about for hours from one inn to another, stopping to drink at all of them. No wonder they were tired out with the worry and his insolence!"

"It appears Miss Descartes has had attacks of fainting like this more than once before. The doctor in Paris thinks there is some weakness of the heart, but forbids her being told," said Mrs Dene.

Ruth interposed quickly, not looking at Gethryn:

"Papa and Monsieur Bordier, where are they?"

"I left them visiting Federl and Sepp in their quarters."

"Well, you will find us in that dreadful little room yonder. It's the only alternative to sitting in the Bauernstube with all the woodchoppers and their bad tobacco, since out of doors fails us. We must go now and make it as pleasant as we can."

Ruth made a motion to go, but Mrs Dene lingered. Her kind eyes, her fair little faded face, were troubled.

"Madame Bordier says the young lady tells her she has met you before, Rex."

"Yes, in Paris"; for his life he could not have kept down the crimson flush that darkened his cheeks and made his temples throb.

Mrs Dene's manner grew a little colder.

"She seems very nice. You knew her people, of course."

"No, I never met any of her people," answered Rex, feeling like a kicked coward. Ruth interposed once more.

"People!" said Ruth, impatiently. "Of course Rex only knows nice people. Come, mother!"

Putting her arm around the old lady, she moved across the hall with decision. As they passed into the cheerless little room, Rex held open the door. Ruth, entering after her mother, looked in his face. It had grown thinner; shadows were deep in the temples; from the dark circles under the eyes to the chin ran a line of pain. She held out her hand to him. He bent and kissed it.

He went and stood in the porch, trying to collect his thoughts. The idea of this meeting between Ruth and Yvonne was insupportable. Why had he not taken means - any, every means to prevent it? He cursed himself. He called himself a coward. He wondered how much Ruth divined. The thought shamed him until his cheeks burned again. And all the while a deep undercurrent of feeling was setting toward that drooping little figure in black, as he had seen it for a moment when she alighted from the carriage and was supported to a room upstairs. Heavens! How it reminded him of that first day in the Place de la Concorde! Why was she in mourning? What did the doctor mean by "weakness of the heart"? What was she doing on mountaintops, and on the stage of a theater if she had heart disease? He started with a feeling that he must go and put a stop to all this folly. Then he remembered the letter. She had told him another man had the right to care for her. Then she was at this moment deserted for the second time, as well as faithless to still another lover! - to how many more? And it was through him that a woman of such a life was brought into contact with Ruth! And Ruth's parents had trusted him; they thought him a gentleman. His brain reeled.

The surging waves of shame and self-contempt subsided, were forgotten. He heard the wind sough in the Luxembourg trees, he smelled the pink flowering chestnuts, a soft voice was in his ear, a soft touch on his arm, her breath on his cheek, the old, old faces came crowding up. Clifford's laugh rang faintly, Braith's grave voice; odd bits and ends of song floated out from the shadows of that past and through the troubled dream of face and laugh and music, so long, so long passed away, he heard the gentle voice of

Yvonne: "Rex, Rex, be true to me; I will come back!"

"I loved her!" he muttered.

There was a stir, a door opened and shut, voices and steps sounded in the room on his left. He leaned forward a little and looked through the uncurtained window.

It was a bare and dingy room containing only a table, some hard chairs, and an old "Flügel" piano with a long inlaid case.

They sat together at the table. Ruth's back was toward him; she was speaking. Yvonne was in the full light. Her eyes were cast down, and she was nervously plaiting the edge of her little black-bordered handkerchief. All at once she raised her eyes and looked straight at the window. How blue her eyes were!

Rex dropped his face in his hands.

"Oh God! I love her!" he groaned.

"Gute Nacht, gnädige Herrn!"

Sepp and Federl stood in their door with a light. Two figures were coming down from the Jaeger's cottage. Gethryn recognized the colonel and Monsieur Bordier.

At the risk of scrutiny from those cool, elderly, masculine eyes, Rex's manhood pulled itself together. He went back to meet them, and presently they all joined the ladies in the apology for a parlor, where coffee was being served.

Coming in after the older men, Rex found no place left in the little, crowded room, excepting one at the table close beside Yvonne. Ruth was on the other side. He went and took the place, self-possessed and smiling.

Yvonne made a slight motion as if to rise and escape. Only Rex saw it. Yes, one more: Ruth saw it.

"Mademoiselle has studied seriously since I had the honor - "

"Oui, Monsieur."

Her faint voice and timid look were more than Ruth could bear. She leaned forward so as to shield the girl as much as possible, and entered into the lively talk at the other end of the table.

Rex spoke again: "Mademoiselle is quite strong, I trust - the stage - Sugar? Allow me! - As I was saying, the stage is a calling which requires a good constitution." No answer.

"But pardon. If you are not strong, how can you expect to succeed in your career?" persisted Rex. His eyes rested on one frail wrist in its black sleeve. The sight filled him with anger.

"I would make my debut if I knew it would kill me." She spoke at last, low but clearly.

"But why? Mon Dieu!"

"Madame has set her heart on it. She thinks I shall do her credit. She has been good to me, so good!" The sad voice fainted and sank away.

Robert W. Chambers

"One is good to one's pupils when they are going to bring one fame," said Rex bitterly.

"Madame took me when she did not know I had a voice - when she thought I was dying - when I was homeless - two years ago."

"What do you mean?" said Rex sternly, sinking his voice below the pitch of the general conversation. "What did you tell me in your letter? Homeless!"

"I never wrote you any letter." Yvonne raised her blue eyes, startled, despairing, and looked into his for the first time.

"You did not write that you had found a - a home which you preferred to - to - any you had ever had? And that it would be useless to - to offer you any other?"

"I never wrote. I was very ill and could not. Afterward I went to - you. You were gone." Her low voice was heartbreaking to hear.

"When?" Rex could hardly utter a word.

"In June, as soon as I left the hospital."

"The hospital? And your mother?"

"She was dead. I did not see her. Then I was very ill, a long time. As soon as I could, I went to Paris."

"To me?"

"Yes."

"And the letter?"

"Ah!" cried Yvonne with a shudder. "It must have been my sister who did that!"

The room was turning round. A hundred lights were swaying about in a crowd of heads. Rex laid his hand heavily on the table to steady himself. With a strong effort at self-control he had reduced the number of lights to two and got the people back in their places when, with a little burst of French exclamations and laughter, everyone turned to Yvonne, and Ruth, bending over her, took both her hands.

The next moment Monsieur Bordier was leading her to the piano.

A soft chord, other chords, deep and sweet, and then the dear voice:

Oui c'est un rêve,
  Un rêve doux d'amour,
La nuit lui prête son mystére

The chain is forged again. The mists of passion rise thickly, heavily, and blot out all else forever.

Hélène's song ceased. He heard them praise her, and heard "Good nights" and "Au revoirs" exchanged. He rose and stood near the door. Ruth passed him like a shadow. They all remained at the foot of the stairs for a moment, repeating their "Adieus" and "Remercie-ments." He was utterly reckless, but cool enough still to watch for his chance in this confusion of civilities. It came; for one instant he could whisper to her, "I must see you tonight." Then the voices were gone and he stood alone on the porch, the wet wind blowing in his face, his face turned up to a heavy sky covered with black, driving clouds. He could hear the river and the moaning of the trees.

It seemed as if he had stood there for hours, never moving. Then there was a step in the dark hall, on the threshold, and Yvonne lay trembling in his arms.

*

The sky was beginning to show a tint of early dawn when they stepped once more upon the silent porch. The wind had gone down. Clouds were piled up in the west, but the east was clear. Perfect stillness was over everything. Not a living creature was in sight, excepting that far up, across the stream, Sepp and Zimbach were climbing toward the Schinder.

"I must go in now. I must you - child!" said Yvonne in her old voice, smoothing her hair with both hands. Rex held her back.

"My wife?" he said.

"Yes!" She raised her face and kissed him on the lips, then clung to him weeping.

"Hush! hush! It is I who should do that," he murmured, pressing her cheek against his breast.

Once more she turned to leave him, but he detained her.

"Yvonne, come with me and be married today!"

"You know it is impossible. Today! what a boy you are! As if we could!"

"Well then, in a few days - in a week, as soon as possible."

"Oh! my dearest! do not make it so hard for me! How could I desert Madame so? After all she has done for me? When I know all her hopes are set on me; that if I fail her she has no one ready to take my place! Because she was so sure of me, she did not try to bring on any other pupil for next autumn. And last season was a bad one for her and Monsieur. Their debutante failed; they lost money. Behold this child!" she exclaimed, with a rapid return to her old gay manner, "to whom I have explained all this at least a hundred times already, and he asks me why we cannot be married today!"

Then with another quick change, she laid her cheek tenderly against his and murmured:

"I might have died but for her. You would not have me desert her so cruelly, Rex?"

"My love! No!" A new respect mingled with his passion. Yes, she was faithful!

"And now I will go in! Rex, Rex, you are quite as bad as ever! Look at my hair!" She leaned lightly on his shoulder, her old laughing self.

He smiled back sadly.

"Again! After all! You silly, silly boy! And it is such a little while to wait!"

"Belle Hélène is very popular in Paris. The piece may run a long time."

"Rex, I must. Don't make it so hard for me!" Tears filled her eyes.

He kissed her for answer, without speaking.

"Think! think of all she did for me; saved me; fed me, clothed me, taught me when she believed I had only voice and talent enough to support myself by teaching. It was half a year before she and Monsieur began to think I could ever make them any return for their care of me. And all that time she was like a mother to me. And now she has told everyone her hopes of me. If I fail she will be ridiculed. You know Paris. She and Monsieur have enemies who will say there never was any pupil, nor any debut expected. Perhaps she will lose her prestige. The fashion may turn to some other teacher. You know what malice can do with ridicule in Paris. Let me sing for her this once, make her one great success, win her one triumph, and then never, never sing again for any soul but you - my husband!"

Her voice sank at the last words, from its eager pleading, to an exquisite modest sweetness.

"But - if you fail?"

"I shall not fail. I have never doubted that I should have a success. Perhaps it is because for myself I do not care, that I have no fear. When I had lost you - I only thought of that. And now that I have found you again - !"

She clung to him in passionate silence.

"And I may not see your debut?"

"If you come I shall surely fail! I must forget you. I must think only of my part. What do I care for the house full of strange faces? I will make them all rise up and shout my name. But if you were there - Ah! I should have no longer any courage! Promise me to come only on the second night."

"But if you do fail, I may come and take you immediately before Monsieur the Maire?"

"If you please!" she whispered demurely.

And they both laughed, the old happy-children laugh of the Atelier.

"I suppose you are bad enough to hope that I will fail," added she presently, with a little moue.

"Yvonne," said Rex earnestly, "I hope that you will succeed. I know you will, and I can wait for you a few weeks more."

"We have waited for our happiness two years. We will make the happiness of others now first, n'est ce pas?" she whispered.

The sky began to glow and the house was astir. Rex knew how it would soon be talking, but he cared for nothing that the world could do or say.

"Ah! we will be happy! Think of it! A little house near the Parc Monceau, my studio there, Clifford, Elliott, Rowden - Bra - all of them coming again! And it will be my wife who will receive them!"

She placed a little soft palm across his lips.

"Taisez-vous, mon ami! It is too soon! See the morning! I must go. There! yes - one more! - my love, Adieu!"

Sixteen

Fewer tourists and more hunters had been coming to the Lodge of late; the crack of the rifle sounded all day. There was great talk of a hunt which the duke would hold in September, and the colonel and Rex were invited. But though September was now only a few days off, the colonel was growing too restless to wait.

After Yvonne's visit, he and Ruth were much together. It seemed to happen so. They took long walks into the woods, but Ruth seemed to share now her father's aversion to climbing, and Gethryn stalked the deer with only the Jaegers for company.

Ruth and her father used to come home with their arms full of wild flowers - the fair, lovely wild blossoms of Bavaria which sprang up everywhere in their path. The colonel was great company on these expeditions, singing airs from obsolete operas of his youth, and telling stories of La Grange, Brignoli and Amodio, of the Strakosches and Maretzeks, with much liveliness. Sometimes there would be a silence, however, and then if Ruth looked up she often met his eyes. Then he would smile and say:

"Well, Daisy!" and she would smile and say:

"Well, dear!"

But this could not last. About a week after Yvonne's visit, the colonel, after one of these walks, instead of joining Rex for a smoke, left him sitting with Ruth under the beech tree and mounted the stairs to Mrs Dene's room.

It was an hour later when he rose and kissed his wife, who had been sitting at her window all the time of their quiet talk, with eyes fixed on the young people below.

"I never dreamed of it!" said he.

"I did, I wished it," was her answer. "I thought he was - but they are all alike!" she ended sadly and bitterly. "To think of a boy as wellborn as Rex - " But the colonel, who possibly knew more about wellborn boys than his wife did, interrupted her:

"Hang the boys! It's Ruth I'm grieved for!"

"My daughter needs no one's solicitude, not even ours!" said the old lady haughtily.

"Right! Thank God!" said the veteran, in a tone of relief. "Good night, my dear!"

Two days later they left for Paris.

Rex accompanied them as far as Schicksalsee, promising to follow them in a few days.

The handsome, soldierly-looking Herr Förster stood by their carriage and gave them a "Glück-liche Reise!" and a warm "Auf Wiedersehen!" as they drove away.

Returning up the steps slowly and seriously, he caught the eye of Sepp and Federl, who had been looking after the carriage as it turned out of sight beyond the bridge:

"Schade!" said the Herr Förster, and went into the house.

"Schade!" said Federl.

"Jammer-schade!" growled Sepp.

On the platform at Schicksalsee, Rex and Ruth were walking while they waited for the train. "Ruth," said Rex, "I hope you never will need a friend's life to save yours from harm; but if you do, take mine."

"Yes, Rex." She raised her eyes and looked into the distance. Far on the horizon loomed the Red Peak.

The clumsy mail drew up beside the platform. It was the year when all the world was running after a very commonplace Operetta with one lovely stolen song: a Volks-song. One heard it everywhere, on both continents; and now as the postillion, in his shiny hat with the cockade, his light blue jacket and white small clothes, and his curly brass horn, came rattling down the street, he was playing the same melody:

Es ist im Leben häßlich eingerichtet -

The train drew into the station. When it panted forth again, Gethryn stood waving his hand, and watched it out of sight.

Turning at last to leave the platform, he found that the crowd had melted away; only a residue of

Robert W. Chambers

crimson-capped officials remained. He inquired of one where he could find an expressman and was referred to a mild man absorbing a bad cigar. With him Gethryn arranged for having his traps brought from Trauerbach and consigned to the brothers Schnurr at the "Gasthof zur Post," Schicksalsee, that inn being close to the station.

This settled, he lighted a cigarette and strolled across to his hotel, sitting down on a stone bench before the door, and looking off at the lake.

It was mid-afternoon. The little place was asleep. Nothing was stirring about the inn excepting a bandy Dachshund, which came wheezing up and thrust a cold nose into the young man's hand. High in the air a hawk was wheeling; his faint, querulous cry struck Gethryn with an unwonted sense of loneliness. He noticed how yellow some of the trees were on the slopes across the lake. Autumn had come before summer was ended. He leaned over and patted the hound. A door opened, a voice cried, "Ei Dachl! du! Dachl!" and the dog made off at the top of his hobbyhorse gait.

The silence was unbroken except for the harsh cries of the hawk, sailing low now in great circles over the lake. The sun flashed on his broad, burnished wings as he stooped; Gethryn fancied he could see his evil little eyes; finally the bird rose and dwindled away, lost against the mountainside.

He was roused from his reverie by angry voices.

"Cochon! Kerl! Menteur!" cried someone.

The other voice remonstrated with a snarl.

"Bah!" cried the first, "you lie!"

"Alsatians," thought Rex; "what horrible French!"

The snarling began again, but gradually lapsed into whining. Rex looked about him.

The quarreling seemed to come from a small room which opened out of the hotel restaurant. Windows gave from it over the front, but the blinds were down.

"No! No! I tell you! Not one sou! Starve? I hope you will!" cried the first voice, and a stamp set some bottles and glasses jingling.

"Alsatians and Jews!" thought Rex. One voice was unpleasantly familiar to him, and he wondered if Mr Blumenthal spoke French as he did English. Deciding with a careless smile that of course he did, Rex ceased to think of him, not feeling any curiosity to go and see with whom his late fellow-lodger might be quarreling. He sat and watched instead, as he lounged in the sunshine, some smart carriages whirling past, their horses stepping high, the lackeys muffled from the mountain air in winter furs, crests on the panels.

An adjutant in green, with a great flutter of white cock's feathers from his chapeau, sitting up on the box of an equipage, accompanied by flunkies in the royal blue and white of Bavaria, was a more agreeable object to contemplate than Mr Blumenthal, and Gethryn felt as much personal connection with the Prince Regent hurrying home to Munich, from his little hunting visit to the emperor of Austria, as with the wrangling Jews behind the close-drawn blinds of the coffee-room at his back.

The sun was slowly declining. Rex rose and idled into the smoking-room. It was deserted but for the clerk at his desk, a railed enclosure, one side of which opened into the smoking-room, the other side into the hall. Across the hall was a door with "Café - Restaurant," in gilt letters above it. Rex did not enter the café; he sat and dreamed in the empty smoking-room over his cigarette.

But it was lively in the café, in spite of the waning season. A good many of the tables were occupied. At one of them sat the three unchaperoned Miss Dashleighs, in company with three solemn, high-shouldered young officers, enjoying something in tall, slender tumblers which looked hot and smelled spicy. At another table Mr Everett Tweeler and Mrs Tweeler were alternately scolding and stuffing Master Irving Tweeler, who expressed in impassioned tones a desire for tarts.

"Ur - r - ving!" remonstrated Mr Tweeler.

"Dahling!" argued Mrs Tweeler. "If oo eats too many 'ittle cakies then oo tant go home to Salem on the puffy, puffy choo-choo boat."

Old Sir Griffin Damby overheard and snorted.

When Master Tweeler secured his tarts, Sir Griffin blessed the meal with a hearty "damn!"

He did not care for Master Tweeler's nightly stomach aches, but their rooms adjoined. When "Ur - r - ving" reached unmolested for his fourth, Sir Griffin rose violently, and muttering, "Change me room, begad!" waddled down to the door, glaring aggressively at the occupants of the various tables. Near the exit a half suppressed squeal caused him to swing round. He had stepped squarely on the toe of a meager individual, who now sat nursing his foot in bitter dejection.

"Pardon - " began Sir Griffin, then stopped and glared at the sallow-faced person.

Sir Griffin stared hard at the man he had stepped on, and at his female companion.

"Damn it!" he cried. "Keep your feet out of the way, do you hear?" puffed his cheeks, squared his shoulders and snorted himself out of the café.

The yellow-faced man was livid with rage.

"Don't be a fool, Mannie," whispered the woman; "don't make a row - do you know who that is?"

"He's an English hog," spluttered the man with an oath; "he's a cursed hog of an Englishman!"

"Yes, and he knows us. He was at Monaco a few summers ago. Don't forget who turned us out of the Casino."

Emanuel Pick turned a shade more sallow and sank back in his seat.

Neither spoke again for some moments. Presently the woman began to stir the bits of lemon and ice in her empty tumbler. Pick watched her sulkily.

"You always take the most expensive drinks. Why can't you order coffee, as others do?" he snarled.

She glanced at him. "Jew," she sneered.

"All right; only wait! I've come to the end of my rope. I've got just money enough left to get back to Paris - "

"You lie, Mannie!"

He paid no attention to this compliment, but lighted a cigar and dropped the match on the floor, grinding it under his heel.

"You have ten thousand francs today! You lie if you say you have not."

Mr Pick softly dropped his eyelids.

"That is for me, in case of need. I will need it too, very soon!"

His companion glared at him and bit her lip.

"If you and I are to remain dear friends," continued Mr Pick, "we must manage to raise money, somehow. You know that as well as I do."

Still she said nothing, but kept her eyes on his face. He glanced up and looked away uneasily.

"I have seen my uncle again. He knows all about your sister and the American. He says it is only because of him that she refuses the handsome offer."

The woman's face grew tigerish, and she nodded rapidly, muttering, "Ah! yes! Mais oui! the American. I do not forget him!"

"My dear uncle thinks it is our fault that your sister refuses to forget him, which is more to the purpose," sneered Pick. "He says you did not press that offer he made Yvonne with any skill, else she would never have refused it again - that makes four times," he added. "Four times she has refused an establishment and - "

"Pst! what are you raising your voice for?" hissed the woman. "And how is it my fault?" she went on.

"I don't say it is. I know better - who could wish more than we that your sister should become the mistress of my dear rich uncle? But when I tried to tell him just now that we had done our best, he raved at me. He has guessed somehow that they mean to marry. I did not tell him that we too had guessed it. But he said I knew it and was concealing it from him. I asked him for a little money to go on with. Curse him, he would not lend me a sou! Said he never would again - curse him!"

There was a silence while Pick smoked on. The woman did not smoke too because she had no cigarette, and Pick did not offer her any. Presently he spoke again.

"Yes, you certainly are an expensive luxury, under the circumstances. And since you have so mismanaged your fool of a sister's affair, I don't see how the circumstances can improve."

She watched him. "And the ten thousand francs? You will throw me off and enjoy them at your ease?"

He cringed at her tone. "Not enjoy - without you - "

"No," she said coolly, "for I shall kill you."

Mr Pick smiled uncomfortably. "That would please the American," he said, trying to jest, but his hand trembled as he touched the stem of his cigar-holder to shake off the ashes.

A sudden thought leaped into her face. "Why not please - me - instead?" she whispered.

Their eyes met. Her face was hard and bold - his, cowardly and ghastly. She clenched her hands and leaned forward; her voice was scarcely audible. Mr Pick dropped his oily black head and listened.

"He turned me out of his box at the Opera; he struck you - do you hear? he kicked you!"

The Jew's face grew chalky.

"Today he stands between you and your uncle, you and wealth, you and me! Do you understand? Cowards are stupid. You claim Spanish blood. But Spanish blood does not forget insults. Is yours only the blood of a Spanish Jew? Bah! Must I talk? You saw him? He is here. Alive. And he kicked you. And he stands between you and riches, you and me, you and - life!"

They sat silent, she holding him fascinated with her little black eyes. His jaw fallen, the expression of his loose mouth was horrible. Suddenly she thrust her face close to his. Her eyes burned and the blood surged through the distended veins under the cracking rouge. Her lips formed the word, "Tonight!"

Without a word he crept from his seat and followed her

out of the room by a side door.

Gethryn, lounging in the smoking-room meanwhile, was listening with delight to the bellowing of Sir Griffin Damby, who stood at the clerk's desk in the hall.

"Don't contradict me!" he roared - the weak-eyed clerk had not dreamed of doing so - "Don't you contradict me! I tell you it's the same man!"

"But Excellence," entreated the clerk, "we do not know - "

"What! Don't know! Don't I tell you?"

"We will telegraph to Paris - "

"Telegraph to hell! Where's my man? Here! Dawson! Do you remember that infernal Jew at Monaco? He's here. He's in there!" jerking an angry thumb at the café door. "Keep him in sight till the police come for him. If he says anything, kick him into the lake."

Dawson bowed.

The clerk tried to say that he would telegraph instantly, but Sir Griffin barked in his face and snorted his way down the hall, followed by the valet.

Rex, laughing, threw down his cigarette and sauntered over to the clerk.

"Whom does the Englishman want kicked out?"

The clerk made a polite gesture, asking Rex to wait

until he had finished telegraphing. At that moment the postillion's horn heralded the coming of the mail coach, and that meant the speedy arrival of the last western train. Rex forgot Sir Griffin and strolled over to the post office to watch the distribution of the letters and to get his own.

A great deal of flopping and pounding seemed to be required as a preliminary to postal distribution. First the mail bags seemed to be dragged all over the floor, then came a long series of thumps while the letters were stamped, finally the slide was raised and a face the color of underdone pie crust, with little angry eyes, appeared. The owner had a new and ingenious insult for each person who presented himself. The Tweelers were utterly routed and went away not knowing whether there were any letters for them or not. Several valets and ladies' maids exchanged lively but ineffectual compliments with the face in the post office window. Then came Sir Griffin. Rex looked on with interest. What the ill-natured brute behind the grating said, Rex couldn't hear, but Sir Griffin burst out with a roar, "Damnation!" that made everybody jump. Then he stuck his head as far as he could get it in at the little window and shouted - in fluent German, awfully pronounced - "Here! You! It's enough that you're so stupid you don't know what you're about. Don't you try to be impudent too! Hand me those letters!" The official bully handed them over without a word.

Rex took advantage of the lull and stepped to the window. "Any letters for Mr Gethryn?"

"How you spell him?" Rex spelled him.

"Yet once again!" demanded the intelligent person.

Rex wrote it in English and in German script.

"From Trauerbach - yes?"

"Yes."

The man went away, looked through two ledgers, sent for another, made out several sets of blanks, and finally came back to the window, but said nothing.

"Well?" said Rex, pleasantly.

"Well," said the man.

"Anything for me?"

"Nothing for you."

"Kindly look again," said Rex. "I know there are letters for me."

In about ten minutes the man appeared again.

"Well?" said Gethryn.

"Well," said the man.

"Nothing for me?"

"Something." And with ostentatious delay he produced three letters and a newspaper, which Rex took, restraining an impulse to knock him down. After all, the temptation was not very great, presenting itself more as an act of justice than as a personal satisfaction. The truth was, all day long a great gentleness tinged with melancholy had rested on Gethryn's spirit. Nothing seemed to matter very much. And whatever engaged his attention for a moment, it was only for a moment, and then his thoughts returned where they had been all day.

Yvonne, Yvonne! She had not been out of his thoughts since he rose that morning. In a few steps he reached his room and read his letters by the waning daylight.

The first began:

> My Darling - in three more days I shall stand before a Paris audience. I am not one bit nervous. I am perfectly happy. Yesterday at rehearsal the orchestra applauded and Madame Bordier kissed me. Some very droll things happened. Achilles was intoxicated and chased Ajax the Less with a stick. Ajax fled into my dressing room, and although I was not there I told Achilles afterward that I would never forgive him. Then he wept.

The letter ran on for a page more of lively gossip and then, with a sudden change, ended:

> But why do I write these foolish things to you? Ah! you know it is because I am too happy! too happy! and I cannot say what is in my heart. I dare not. It is too soon. I dare not!

> If it is that I am happy, who but you knows the reason? And now listen to my little secret. I pray for you, yes, every morning and every evening. And for myself too - now.

> God forgives. It is in my faith. Oh! my husband, we will be good!

Thy Yvonne

Gethryn's eyes blurred on the page and he sat a long time, very still, not offering to open his remaining letters. Presently he raised his head and looked into the street. It was dusk, and the lamps along the lake side were lighted. He had to light his candles to read by.

The next was from Braith - a short note.

Everything is ready, Rex, your old studio cleaned and dusted until you would not know it.

I have kept the key always by me, and no one but myself has ever entered it since you left.

I will meet you at the station - and when you are really here I shall begin to live again.

Au revoir,
Braith

It seemed as if Gethryn would never get on with his correspondence. He sat and held this letter as he had done the other. A deep melancholy possessed him. He did not care to move. At last, impatiently, he tore the third envelope. It contained a long letter from Clifford.

"My blessed boy," it said.

We learn from Papa Braith that you will be here before long, but the old chump won't tell when. He intends to meet you all alone at the station, and wishes to dispense with a gang and a brass band. We think that's deuced selfish. You are our prodigal as well as his, and we are considering several plans for getting even with Pa.

One is to tell you all the news before he has a chance. And I will begin at once.

Thaxton has gone home, and opened a studio in New York. The Colossus has grown two more inches and hates to hear me mention the freak museums in the Bowery. Carleton is a hubby, and wifey is English and captivating. Rowden told me one day he was going to get married too. When I asked her name he said he didn't know. Someone with red hair.

When I remarked that he was a little in that way himself, he said yes, he knew it, and he intended to found a race of that kind, to be known as the Red Rowdens. Elliott's brindle died, and we sold ours. We now keep two Russian bloodhounds. When you come to my room, knock first, for "Baby" doesn't like to be startled.

Braith has kept your family together, in your old studio. The parrot and the raven are two old fiends and will live forever. Mrs Gummidge periodically sheds litters of kittens, to Braith's indignation. He gives them to the concierge who sells them at a high price, I don't know for what purpose; I have two of the Gummidge children. The bull pups are pups no longer, but they are beauties and no mistake. All the same, wait until you see "Baby."

I met Yvonne in the Louvre last week. I'm glad you are all over that affair, for she's going to be married, she told me. She looked prettier than ever, and as happy as she was pretty. She was with old Bordier of the Fauvette, and his wife, and - think of this! she's coming out in Belle Hélène! Well! I'm glad she's all right, for she was too nice to go the usual way.

Poor little Bulfinch shot himself in the Bois last June. He had delirium tremens. Poor little chap!

There's a Miss Dene here, who knows you. Braith has met her. She's a beauty, he says, and she's also a stunning girl, possessing manners, and morals, and dignity, and character, and religion and all that you and I have not, my son. Braith says she isn't too good for you when you are at your best; but we know better, Reggy; any good girl is too good for the likes of us.

Hasten to my arms, Reginald! You will find them at No. 640 Rue Notre Dame des Champs, chez,

Foxhall Clifford, Esq.

Leaving Clifford's letter and the newspapers on the table, Rex took his hat, put out the light, and went down to the street. As he stood in the door, looking off at the dark lake, he folded Yvonne's letter and placed it in his breast. He held Braith's a moment more and then laid it beside hers.

The air was brisk; he buttoned his coat about him. Here and there a moonbeam touched the lapping edge of the water, or flashed out in the open stretch beyond the point of pines. High over the pines hung a cliff, blackening the water all around with fathomless shadow.

A waiter came lounging by, his hands tucked beneath his coattails. "What point is that? The one which overhangs the pines there?" asked Rex.

"Gracious sir!" said the waiter, "that is the Schicksalfels."

"Why `Schicksal-fels'?"

"Has the gracious gentleman never heard the legend of the `Rock of Fate'?"

"No, and on second thoughts, I don't care to hear it now. Another time. Good night!"

"Ah! the gentleman is too good! Thousand thanks! Gute Nacht, gnädiger Herr!"

Gethryn remained looking at the crags.

"They cannot be half a mile from here," he thought. "I suppose the path is good enough; if not, I can turn back. The lake will look well from there by moonlight." And he found himself moving up a little footpath which branched below the hotel.

It was pleasant, brisk walking. The air had a touch of early frost in it. Gethryn swung along at a good pace, pulling his cap down and fastening the last button of his coat. The trees threw long shadows across the path, hiding it from view, except where the moonlight fell white on the moist gravel. The moon herself was past the full and not very bright; a film of mist was drawing over the sky. Gethryn, looking up, thought of that gentle moon which once sailed ghostlike at high noon through the blue zenith among silver clouds while a boy lay beside the stream with rod and creel; and then he remembered the dear old yellow moon that used to flood the nursery with pools of light and pile strange moving shades about his bed. And then he saw, still looking up, the great white globe that hung above the frozen river, striking blue sparks from the ringing skates.

He felt lonely and a trifle homesick. For the first time in his life - he was still so young - he thought of his childhood and his boyhood as something gone beyond recall.

He had nearly reached his destination; just before him the path entered a patch of pine woods and emerged from it, shortly, upon the flat-topped rock which he was seeking. Under the first arching branches he stopped and looked back at the marred moon in the mist-covered sky.

"I am sick of this wandering," he thought. "Wane quickly! Your successor shall shine on my home: Yvonne's and mine."

And, thinking of Yvonne, he passed into the shadows which the pines cast upon the Schicksalfels.

Seventeen

Paris lay sparkling under a cold, clear sky. The brilliant streets lay coiled along the Seine and stretched glittering from bank to bank, from boulevard to boulevard; cafés, brasseries, concert halls and theaters in the yellow blaze of gas and the white and violet of electricity.

It was not late, but people who entered the lobby of the Theater Fauvette turned away before the placard "Standing room only."

Somewhere in the city a bell sounded the hour, and with the last stroke the drop curtain fell on the first act of "La Belle Hélène."

It fell amidst a whirlwind of applause, in which the orchestra led.

The old leader of the violins shook his head, however. He had been there twenty years, and he had never before heard of such singing in comic opera.

"No, no," he said, "she can't stay here. Dame! she sings!"

Madame Bordier was pale and happy; her good

husband was weak with joy. The members of the troupe had not yet had time to be jealous and they, too, applauded.

As for the house, it was not only conquered, it was wild with enthusiasm. The lobbies were thronged.

Braith ran up against Rowden and Elliott.

"By Jove!" they cried, with one voice, "who'd have thought the little girl had all that in her? I say, Braith, does Rex know about her? When is he coming?"

"Rex doesn't know and doesn't care. Rex is cured," said Braith. "And he's coming next week. Where's Clifford?" he added, to make a diversion.

"Clifford promised to meet us here. He'll be along soon."

The pair went out for refreshments and Braith returned to his seat.

The wait between the acts proved longer than was agreeable, and people grumbled. The machinery would not work, and two heavy scenes had to be shifted by hand. Good Monsieur Bordier flew about the stage in a delirium of excitement. No one would have recognized him for the eminently reasonable being he appeared in private life. He called the stage hands "Prussian pigs!" and "Spanish cattle!" and expressed his intention to dismiss the whole force tomorrow.

Yvonne, already dressed, stood at the door of her room, looking along the alley of dusty scenery to where a warm glow revealed the close proximity of the

Robert W. Chambers

footlights. There was considerable unprofessional confusion, and not a little skylarking going on among the company, who took advantage of the temporary interruption.

Yvonne stood in the door of her dressing room and dreamed, seeing nothing.

Her pretty figure was draped in a Grecian tunic of creamy white, bordered with gold; her soft, dark hair was gathered in a simple knot.

Presently she turned and entered her dressing room, closing the door. Then she sat down before the mirror, her chin resting on her hands, her eyes fixed on her reflected eyes, a faint smile curving her lips.

"Oh! you happy girl!" she thought. "You happy, happy girl! And just a little frightened, for tomorrow he will come. And when he says - for he will say it - `Yvonne must we wait?' I shall tell him, No! take me now if you will!"

Without a knock the door burst open. A rush of music from the orchestra came in. Yvonne thought "So they have begun at last!" The same moment she rose with a faint, heartsick cry. Her sister closed the door and fastened it, shutting out all sound but that of her terrible voice. Yvonne blanched as she looked on that malignant face. With a sudden faintness she leaned back, pressing one hand to her heart.

"You received my letter?" said the woman.

Yvonne did not answer. Her sister stamped and came nearer. "Speak!" she cried.

Yvonne shrank and trembled, but kept her resolute eyes on the cruel eyes approaching hers.

"Shall I tear an answer from you?" said the woman, always coming nearer. "Do you think I will wait your pleasure, now?"

No answer.

"He is here - Mr Blumenthal; he is waiting for you. You dare not refuse him again! You will come with us now, after the opera. Do you hear? You will come. There is no more time. It must be now. I told you there would be time, but there is none - none!"

Yvonne's maid knocked at the door and called:

"Mademoiselle, c'est l'heuer!"

"Answer!" hissed the woman.

Yvonne, speechless, holding both hands to her heart, kept her eyes on her sister's face. That face grew ashen; the eyes had the blank glare of a tiger's; she sprang up to Yvonne and grasped her by the wrists.

"Mademoiselle! Mademoiselle! c'est l'heure!" called the maid, shaking the door.

"Fool!" hissed her sister, "you think you will marry the American!"

"Mademoiselle Descartes! mais Mademoiselle Descartes!" cried Monsieur's voice without.

"Let me go!" panted Yvonne, struggling wildly.

"Go!" screamed the woman, "go, and sing! You cannot marry him! He is dead!" and she struck the girl with her clenched fist.

The door, torn open, crashed behind her and immediately swung back again to admit Madame.

"My child! my child! What is it? What ails you? Quick, or it will be too late! Ah! try, try, my child!"

She was in tears of despair.

Taking her beseeching hand, Yvonne moved toward the stage.

"Oui, chère Madame!" she said.

The chorus swelled around her.

Oh! reine en ce jour!

rose, fell, ebbed away, and left her standing alone.

She heard a voice - "Tell me, Venus - " but she hardly knew it for her own. It was all dark before her eyes - while the mad chorus of Kings went on, "For us, what joy!" - thundering away along the wings.

"Fear Calchas!"

"Seize him!"

"Let Calchas fear!"

And then she began to sing - to sing as she had never sung before. Sweet, thrilling, her voice poured forth into the crowded auditorium. The people sat spell-bound. There was a moment of silence; no one offered to applaud. And then she began again.

Oui c'est un réve,
Un réve doux d'amour -

She faltered -

La nuit lui préte son mystère,
Il doit finir avec le jour -

the voice broke. Men were standing up in the audience. One cried out:

"Il - doit - finir - "

The music clashed in one great discord.

Why did the stage reel under her? What was the shouting?

Her heavy, dark hair fell down about her little white face as she sank on her knees, and covered her as she lay her slender length along the stage.

The orchestra and the audience sprang to their feet. The great blank curtain rattled to the ground. A whirlwind swept over the house. Monsieur Bordier stepped before the curtain.

"My friends!" he began, but his voice failed, and he only added, "C'est fini!"

With hardly a word the audience moved to the exits. But Braith, turning to the right, made his way through a long, low passage and strode toward a little stage door. It was flung open and a man hurried past him.

"Monsieur!" called Braith. "Monsieur!"

But Monsieur Bordier was crying like a child, and kept on his way,
without answering.

The narrow corridor was now filled with hurrying, excited figures in gauze and tinsel, sham armor, and painted faces. They pressed Braith back, but he struggled and fought his way to the door.

A Sergeant de Ville shouldered through the crowd. He was dragging a woman along by the arm. Another policeman came behind, urging her forward. Somehow she slipped from them and sank, cowering against the wall. Braith's eyes met hers. She cowered still lower.

A slender, sallow man had been quietly slipping through the throng. A red-faced fellow touched him on the shoulder.

"Pardon! I think this is Mr Emanuel Pick."

"No!" stammered the man, and started to run.

Braith blocked his way. The red-faced detective was at his side.

"So, you are Mr Emanuel Pick!"

"No!" gasped the other.

"He lies! He lies!" yelled the woman, from the floor.

The Jew reeled back and, with a piercing scream, tore at his handcuffed wrists. Braith whispered to the detective:

"What has the woman done? What is the charge?"

"Charge? There are a dozen. The last is murder."

The woman had fainted and they carried her away. The light fell a moment on the Jew's livid face, the next Braith stood under the dark porch of the empty theater. The confusion was all at the stage entrance. Here, in front, the deserted street was white and black and silent under the electric lamps. All the lonelier for two wretched gamins, counting their dirty sous and draggled newspapers.

When they saw Braith they started for him; one was ahead in the race, but the other gained on him, reached him, dealt him a merciless blow, and panted up to Braith.

The defeated one, crying bitterly, gathered up his scattered papers from the gutter.

"Curse you, Rigaud! you hound!" he cried, in a passion of tears. "Curse you, son of a murderer!"

The first gamin whipped out a paper and thrust it toward Braith.

"Buy it, Monsieur!" he whined, "the last edition, full account of the Boulangist riot this morning; burning of the Prussian flags; explosion on a warship; murder in Germany, discovered by an English Milord - "

Braith was walking fast; the gamin ran by his side for a moment, but soon gave it up. Braith walked faster and faster; he was almost running when he reached his own door. There was a light in his window. He rushed up the stairs and into his room.

Clifford was sitting there, his head in his hands. Braith touched him, trying to speak lightly.

"Are you asleep, old man?"

Clifford raised a colorless face to his.

"What is it? Can't you speak?"

But Clifford only pointed to a crumpled telegram lying on the table, and hid his face again as Braith raised the paper to the light.

*